THE SELF-LIBERATION OF PARSON SYKES

Return to Southampton County

David J. Mason

Published By

HMG ePublishing LLC

Princeton, New Jersey 08540

Library of Congress Control Number: 2025919203

ISBN13: 978-0-9991331-6-3

ISBN10: 0-9991331-6-0

Printed in the United States of America

Copyright © 2025 by David J. Mason

Disclaimer

The publication, The Self-Liberation of Parson Sykes Trilogy, is a documentary novel based on a true story and actual events and was drawn from a variety of sources, including published materials and interviews. For dramatic and narrative purposes, the play contains fictionalized scenes, composite and representative characters and dialogue, and time compression. The views and opinions expressed in the novel are those of the characters only and do not necessarily reflect or represent the views and opinions held by individuals on which those characters are based.

Published by

HMG ePublishing, LLC

Princeton, New Jersey 08540

hello@hmg-e-publishing.com

Foreword

The *Self-Liberation of Parson Sykes: Return to Southampton County* is the third novel in the *Self-Liberation of Sykes Trilogy*. Growing up with my cousin David, I was always amazed by anecdotes of our great-grandfather in Southampton County, Virginia. Our family reunions always included discussions about his heroic escape from enslavement, bringing together relatives of all ages. Despite spanning more than 150 years, this ongoing saga continues to affect other family members. As a Parson's descendants, proprietor, a retired educator, and former School Board Chair of Norfolk, Virginia, I am honored to provide this foreword.

Along with David, I became interested in the history of the Sykes family early in life while attending family reunions and hearing stories of his mother's ancestors from Southampton County, Virginia. For over 150 years, Parson Sykes' descendants passed down stories and adventures of Parson's early life at family reunions, holiday meals, weddings, and other gatherings where the ancestors met.

This story is not just a historical account, but a gripping, family-inspired narrative that will motivate, educate, and connect relatives with the principles of the American constitutional republic. A trilogy, David's story profiles Private Parson Sykes' evolution from enslavement in Southampton County, Virginia, followed by his enlistment into the Union Army, and culminating with his emancipation and return to the county.

The way David arranged this true and traditional family story comes through as a riveting story from start to finish. *Return to Southampton County* took place from April 1865 to January 1870, following the American Civil War, at the Union Army encampment in City Point, Virginia. Although racism and discrimination resulted in ongoing oppression for Black Americans, Parson believed that his military service in the Union Army would earn him trust and respect, at least within his family. The book is the story of Parson's journey back home and the challenges he encountered.

A Civil War and Black history enthusiast, David researched our great-grandfather's military service and wrote *The Self-Liberation of Parson Sykes* based on his findings. David writes with authenticity, attention to detail, and cares about subjects that are sensitive to many people, presenting the facts as they are. He paints a clear picture of people and events that made me feel closer to Parson Sykes as I read the book. I am fascinated to know the historical details of the brave actions our great-grandfather undertook.

Again, I am honored to write this foreword. I hope that each family member and every other reader will appreciate this outstanding story of the determination, strength, and faith of our family.

Yours Truly,

Ulysses Turner
Norfolk, Virginia
November 1, 2025

Preface

In this book, the third installment of the trilogy, I examine the history of the Reconstruction Era, spanning from 1863 to 1870, and offer a fresh perspective on the concept of practical freedom. This self-liberation project aims to provide an enjoyable, practical guide to Black history and genealogy, offering real-world examples and models. This book is not intended to be a definitive history, but rather a collection of interesting historical stories and reflections on the path to freedom during the Reconstruction era.

Return to Southampton County is the third documentary novel in the *Self-Liberation of Parson Sykes* trilogy. The concept of birthright citizenship grabbed my attention, and I began drafting this book to explore its roots. I felt the need to memorialize my ancestors' journey and wisdom. Having spent five decades researching my genealogy and Black history, I felt a responsibility to share my findings and contribute to the ongoing conversation.

As a civil war enthusiast with thirty years of experience in the United States Army, I have seen firsthand the impact of the Reconstruction Era on human and civil rights. This book is based on years of research, including Federal government records and archives, as well as interviews with family members, which provide a unique perspective on the results of Reconstruction. While authoring this book, digital access to valuable governmental, academic, and private sources of historical and genealogical information proved to be an invaluable resource for me.

In the trilogy, the readers will find practical advice, historical anecdotes, and information that will help them apply the concepts discussed in this book. The trilogy's careful attention to historical detail, referencing major historical events, makes it a valuable resource on the journey of Black Americans from enslavement to emancipation.

I intended this book to be accessible to both experts and those new to the aims and results of the Reconstruction era. It offers a point of view from those who lived through the violent pogroms, political turmoil, and the intrinsic insurrection that permeated the nation. I encourage readers to approach this book with an open mind and to engage with the ideas presented, as they should spark their discussion.

Use the anecdotes of Black historical and genealogical events as leads to explore the legacy of Black Americans' humanitarian and civil rights gains during Reconstruction more deeply. Hopefully, the story of Parson Sykes's resilience and transformation from an enslaved teenager to a combat veteran, landowner, and settlement advocate will serve as an inspiration for others.

David J. Mason
Skillman, New Jersey
November 1, 2025

Introduction

Between 1863 and 1877, the nation undertook the obligation of integrating formerly enslaved people into a bitterly divided country over emancipation. During this era, referred to as Reconstruction, the Federal government phased in initiatives to reunite the country and address the issues of emancipation. The era witnessed the monumental legal abolition of enslavement, the extension of citizenship, and voting rights to Black American men. However, these revolutionary changes were resisted, widening the gap between legal rights and the realities of violence, economic control, and inequality for formerly enslaved citizens.

Return to Southampton County, book three in the trilogy, narrates the experiences of freed people in the era, examining their efforts to establish schools, acquire land, and participate in the political process. With the digitization of the Freedmen's Bureau records, I had access to a firsthand perspective on the Reconstruction period, including information on government policies and the dealings between formerly enslaved people and officials. Drawing on these sources, I will demonstrate how the pursuit of practical freedom, despite legal guarantees, often meant navigating political betrayal and violent white supremacy.

Amid the Civil War, the nation grappled with defining freedom, a concept profoundly shaped by the emancipation of millions. At President Lincoln's strong behest and with his active encouragement, the Republican Party fulfilled the momentous task of drafting the Thirteenth Amendment to the United States Constitution. The House of Representatives passed the amendment on January 31, 1865, and President Lincoln signed it and then sent it to the states for ratification. Yet, as the ink dried on the document, a new battle began. The fight for actual, practical freedom often stood in stark contrast to the legal declarations that promise it.

Initially, ratification seemed assured, with nineteen states voting for the amendment by the end of March. However, by April 14, 1865, the date of President Lincoln's assassination, only twenty-one states had ratified the amendment.

This book argues that while legal emancipation provided a foundational shift, the practical attainment of freedom for Black Americans during Reconstruction remained elusive. This disparity, shaped by economic hardship, racial violence, and political maneuvering, hindered the promise of a truly inclusive democracy and laid the groundwork for a century of racial injustice. It informs readers of the daunting task that America faced in restoring order in the South, reunifying a war-torn nation, and extending equality to Black Americans.

By unraveling the intricate interplay between legal rights and lived realities, this book aims to deepen our understanding of freedom itself. It urges us to consider what it truly means to be free – politically, socially, and economically. However, Black Americans made gains during Reconstruction. Through actual or threatened anti-Black violence, the control of southern society was returned to those committed to restoring and maintaining white domination. Researching the unfinished revolution of Reconstruction offers critical lessons for understanding the enduring challenges of racial inequality in America today.

By examining the core conflicts and historical issues of Reconstruction, I gained valuable insights into the roots of current problems, such as systemic racism, voter suppression, and economic inequality. This includes the rise of Black political power, white supremacist resistance, and the eventual withdrawal of federal protection for Black citizens. Studying the successes and failures of Reconstruction allows me to recognize the gap between the promise of legal emancipation and the lived reality of practical freedom.

Beyond addressing the painful gap between promise and reality, I aimed to highlight the human spirit's resilience against dehumanization and the vigilance required to overcome it. While a laudable resolution, it does not erase the struggle for a hard-won, deeply meaningful victory.

If you enjoy detailed, well-researched historical accounts that humanize sweeping historical events through the lens of a single, fascinating individual, you will find this book incredibly rewarding.

Contents

Prologue

Dawn of Reconstruction

Parson Sykes had never known a night so cold, nor a silence so deadly, as the night he and his brothers ran. Even years later, he could still feel the way the December 1864 air burned in his lungs, and the muddy banks of the Black River pressed hard against his back. There was no moon to guide them—only the distant echo of dogs barking, and the knowledge that if they were caught, mercy would not be on offer.

He was seventeen. He had grown up in a Virginia where the law was written in a language that meant nothing to him except "no." No rights, no justice, no chance. Every day was a lesson drilled in by masters and codebooks, designed to keep people like him ignorant and afraid. But tonight, he had something stronger than fear: the taste of freedom, sharp and exhilarating, right there on the other side of the water.

The escape had been Joseph's idea. Henry—always the steady one—had tried to talk them out of it more than once, but Parson could see even he was tired of waiting for someone else to declare him human. They moved in silence, keeping low, every branch a threat and every gust of wind a warning. When the three brothers reached the riverbank, Parson risked a glance back. The plantation was just a smear of shadow on the horizon, but he could feel Jacob Williams' eyes on him—the old man who had owned him, who'd taught him that hope was dangerous, that freedom was a kind of madness.

They had made it only halfway across the river's edge when the dogs came howling. Two bounty hunters, rifles glinting in the thin dawn, stepped out from behind the brush. Parson could feel his heart pounding so hard he thought it might give them away. He remembered the stories the elders told, what happened to runaways when they were dragged back, the scars, the missing fingers, the way whole families disappeared for asking too many questions. But the hunters made a mistake: they thought they had caught three frightened boys. Parson's hands shook as he pretended to plead, but inside he was calculating, waiting for the right moment. When it came, the brothers moved as one—a flash of fists, a scramble in the mud, the crack of a jaw breaking. They did not look back.

By the time the sun rose, they were east of the river, their clothes soaked and their bodies aching. It was not over. Every step was a gamble. Every stranger's face could mean betrayal. The war had turned Virginia inside out; soldiers and spies and desperate men crowded every road. The brothers stumbled onward in the direction of Norfolk County, drawn by rumors— whispers of Union troops, of Lincoln's proclamation, of a new world being born in blood and smoke.

They reached the Federal lines at daybreak. The pickets wore blue and carried themselves like men who could not be bought. These were the United States Colored Troops, Company I, 1st Cavalry Regiment. They did not ask questions. They offered a rifle and a uniform, and Parson seized the chance. He would fight, not just to survive, but to claim a life that had always been denied him.

Training at Camp Hamilton was brutal. The officers barked orders as if they could sweat the enslavement out of a man, and there were nights when Parson thought he might break. But he learned quickly. He learned that freedom was earned inch by inch, that dignity could be built from nothing but hunger and rage. He remembered his mother, Louisa, back at Southampton—her hands stained with cherry juice, her wild cherry syrup simmering on the fire, the only medicine against the exhaustion and terror that pressed down on them all. Parson searched for those cherries along the riverbanks, their dark sweetness a reminder of home, of the small acts of resistance that kept his family alive.

The war had its own rhythm. Patrols, drills, and skirmishes along the James River. Parson saw men die for a country that had treated them as livestock, and he felt something inside him harden. He carried the memory of Nat Turner's rebellion like a hidden scar. He had been a child when he first heard the stories—how Turner's uprising had turned Southampton County into a war zone, how the blood of sixty white families, including Jacob Williams' wife and children, had brought down a punishment on every Black man, woman, and child. The insurrection had ended, but the laws that followed were worse than chains. Parson had watched neighbors disappear, seen his own father, Solomon, grow thin and silent under the weight of suspicion. The state made it illegal to teach a Black child to read, illegal to gather, and illegal to hope.

All of it pressed down on him now: the history, the fear, the absolute certainty that if he failed, there would be no second chance. Jacob Williams had made it clear—freedom was an illusion, emancipation a trick. Even after Lincoln's proclamation in 1863, the old man clung to Parson like a shadow, determined to keep him in a state of near-slavery, to deny him rights, land, or dignity. Parson's only answer was to run harder, fight longer, and want more.

He marched with the Union Army as the war turned against the Confederacy. He saw the wild cherry trees bloom along the banks, the same trees that had sheltered him as a child. He remembered the syrup his mother made for the family, a secret recipe sweetened with honey and spiked with his father's hidden whiskey. Sometimes, in his barracks at Fort Burnham, Parson would close his eyes and see Louisa's hands, the steam rising from her pot, the taste of cherries on his tongue. Every victory by the Union felt like another promise kept, another step toward the life he had been denied.

Yet nothing was certain. As the Confederate lines broke and the Union marched into Richmond, Parson realized that freedom was not a finish line but a beginning. He saw the confusion and bitterness in the air—soldiers unsure of what came next, politicians arguing over who belonged and who did not. President Lincoln, lionized by some and hated by others, made plans to reunite the country, but Parson saw the cracks. There was no shared vision, no easy path to true equality. Reconstruction brought with it a different kind of danger, a new fight for rights that were still only words on paper.

The war changed Parson. He had left Southampton County as a runaway, a boy marked by self-doubt and fear, shaped by the humiliation and violence of chattel slavery. In battle, he found a new strength, but also a new set of wounds—wounds that did not heal with time. He became a soldier, then a man, and yet the ache of what he had lost, of what had been stolen from him, never quite faded.

He knew the stakes. He had seen what happened to those who reached for too much, who wanted more than survival. He had watched men broken for the crime of wanting land, women punished for the audacity to learn. Parson wanted everything: the right to vote, to own land, to stand equal before the law, to walk through Southampton County as a free man and not a shadow. He wanted to see his parents again, to taste his mother's syrup, to plant something of his own in Virginia soil and watch it grow.

Night after night, as the war wound down, Parson felt the weight of the future pressing in. He saw the glances exchanged by the old masters, the way they tightened their grip on power, the rumors of new codes and old hatreds returning. He knew he could not afford to fail—not for himself, not for his family, not for the thousands who had run, fought, and died for a promise that was still unfinished.

In those moments, Parson's hands would tremble, and the fear of capture would creep up his spine, as sharp and real as it had been the night he fled. But he pressed on. He learned to forgive his own mistakes, to see his flaws not as shameful but as scars earned in the fight for something better. He made himself a promise: he would not just survive, he would claim the fullness of his freedom. He would not let Jacob Williams, or the laws of Virginia, or the bitter legacy of the insurrection, define the limits of his life.

So, when Richmond fell on April 2, 1865, and Black soldiers marched through the city's battered streets, Parson Sykes held his head high. He was no longer just an escaped slave. He was a witness, a survivor, a man remaking himself in the ruins of a broken country. He had risked everything for a future that was still uncertain, but it was his. For the first time, he felt the ground solid beneath his feet, the air sweet with the promise of spring, and the wild cherry trees along the James River ready to blossom again.

He knew the struggle was far from over. The old fears lingered, and the new world was fragile. But Parson's journey—from the banks of the Black River to the heart of the war—had taught him that freedom was both a prize and a burden. It required courage not just to run, but to return, to rebuild, to insist on dignity even when the world offered none.

Every step he took was a step away from the past, a step toward a future he would shape himself, no matter what the cost. And as the cherry trees bloomed and the river ran free, Parson Sykes understood at last that the fight for freedom was his alone to finish—and that he was ready.

Lincoln stated in the Gettysburg Address that the nation fought the Civil War for the preservation of freedom. This declaration instilled hope in Parson. At Fort Burnham, Parson read the *Philadelphia Inquirer* and learned about Lincoln's Gettysburg Address. The address opened Parson's insight to a world beyond Southampton County and expanded the sphere of his self-liberation ordeal. It stated that the soldiers' sacrifices were not in vain and conveyed a unifying message about the country's purpose, even in the face of considerable human loss.

Lincoln's message inspired hope in Parson by reaffirming the determination of self-liberation after the Civil War. As he recalled, the proclamation's promise of freedom relied on the Federal military victories and the contributions of Black service members who fought for the country and freedom.

The Gettysburg Address established that the war to save the nation would also be a war for freedom. It added moral force to the federal cause and strengthened the Union both militarily and politically. The challenge of abolishing enslavement after the war went beyond simply ending the legal practice. It also involved tackling the deeply entrenched social and economic structures that depended on enslaved Black labor.

Although Lincoln did not live to see the end of enslavement in the entire country, his Gettysburg Address captured Parson's heart and imagination. It gave him hope and the will to continue his self-liberation journey after the Civil War.

On February 3, 1865, President Lincoln and his Secretary of State, William Henry Seward, hosted the Hampton Roads Peace Conference. This meeting represented an attempt to negotiate a peace settlement to end the Civil War. As the country entered the fourth year of the Civil War, with the ongoing devastation to its economy, landscape, and psyche, Abraham Lincoln was desperate for peace and an end to suffering. The war had been raging for almost four years, with daily expenditures reaching $3 million at this point. The war-fatigued country yearned for resolution and an end to the conflict.

In search of a way to end the Civil War, the peace conference convened at Fort Monroe, Virginia. The Confederate envoys included the Confederate Vice President Alexander Stephens, Assistant Secretary of War John Campbell, and Virginia Senator Robert Hunter. Their faces showed the same longing and the strain of the past four years. From the shore, Parson witnessed the men go aboard the River Queen steamship, anchored in Hampton Roads, Virginia, near Fort Monroe.

Lincoln, thinking ahead to reconciliation, hoped to ease the people of the Confederacy into post-war Reconstruction. The most significant shift for the country and the former Confederate states would be the emancipation of four million enslaved people. At this conference, Lincoln conveyed his vision for a swift transition to emancipation, believing it would accelerate peace.

He pledged to the Confederate envoy that he would be generous in restoring property taken under the Confiscation Act, passed July 17, 1862. By contrast, Lincoln said, "People enslaved by civilian and military Confederate officials shall be forever free." However, it was enforceable only in the former Confederate states occupied by the Federal Army.

During the conference, Lincoln considered revisiting the Compensated Emancipation Act of 1862, which provided $300 in reparations for each enslaved person freed in the District of Columbia. The cost of buying each enslaved person from the people who enslaved them would be less than the staggering cost of the war. He offered the Act in return for laying down the Confederate arms, the lives, liberty, and property of all Southerners, and an agreeable post-war order.

The Confederate diplomats counter-proposed a scheme in which Lee and his Army retreated from Richmond into Mexico, which Grant and the Federal armies pursued. Reunion would follow, and the two forces would join to fight the Emperor of Mexico. The South would abandon enslavement for a chance to take Mexico, and Jefferson Davis would become President of Mexico. Lincoln clearly expressed his disinterest in invading Mexico and provoking an international conflict. Despite Lincoln's surprising offer to buy each enslaved person from their enslavers, the five negotiators did not come to a peace agreement.

Leading up to the peace conference, President Lincoln began conceptualizing his Proclamation of Amnesty and Reconstruction policy. Known as the Ten-Percent Plan, it aimed at integrating formerly enslaved people into a sharply divided country. Lincoln himself took a pragmatic approach to Reconstruction, insisting only that the Southerners pledge future loyalty to the Union and emancipate their enslaved people. He viewed this approach as an initial step toward ending the conflict and solidifying white support for abolition. Since the war was still ongoing, his policy was a plausible notion and not intended as a blueprint for Reconstruction.

By April 1865, Louisiana, Arkansas, Tennessee, and Virginia formed loyal governments under Lincoln's plan. They sought readmission to the Union by seating their senators and representatives in Congress. The most vigorous of these appointees was Andrew Johnson, a War Democrat, who effectively reconstituted a loyal government in Tennessee. This success led to his nomination as Vice President on the Republican ticket with Lincoln in 1864.

Earlier, in 1864, the Republicans contended that their National Union Party was for all loyal men. Although an honest and honorable man, Andrew Johnson was one of the least qualified and unprepared individuals to assume the Presidency. Johnson never attended school, but he taught himself to read, write, and memorize the United States Constitution. He married Eliza McCardle in 1827, and she subsequently educated him. Johnson, a gifted orator, quickly ascended the political ladder.

With Johnson nominated for Vice President, the Radical Republicans won an overwhelming victory in the Congressional elections that fall. As the Federal Army subdued former Confederate states, Lincoln appointed military governors to supervise their restoration and readmission.

Upon Andrew Johnson's ascension to the Vice Presidency, stories regarding the public executions of USCT soldiers and racial tensions began to resurface. Given Vice President Johnson's deep-seated prejudices against Black people, the stories led to isolated episodes of disorders, a lack of discipline, and lower morale. A self-made person, he had opposed enslavement mainly because it gave advantages to the Southern aristocrats. Unlike Lincoln, he had little empathy for the enslaved people themselves. He was perfectly willing for their new status to be defined by those who had supervised them in the years before the war.

In the Federal Army, the public execution of USCT soldiers seemed typical. However, the execution cases were individual, and there was no evidence of preconceived action. The War Department directed that those men convicted of desertion were "to be shot to death with musketry, at such time and place as the commanding General may direct." Federal Army firing squads executed several alleged deserters in the spring of 1864 and remained active until the evacuations of Richmond and Petersburg.

An example of the type of stories that were recirculated through USCT regiments was a report cited in the *Richmond Daily Dispatch*. According to the report of September 10, 1864, a Black soldier in the Federal Army in Petersburg attempted to rape a white woman whose husband was serving in the Confederate Army. Authorities caught this Black soldier, named William Johnson of the 23rd Infantry Regiment, USCT, then tried him by court-martial, found him guilty, and sentenced him to hang. The Confederate Army, under a flag of truce, requested permission to hang Johnson in plain sight of both armies between the lines. Authorities granted the request, and a newspaper published a photograph of the hanging.

Before the assembled regiment, the officer of the day read his offense and his sentence. The prisoner, under escort, followed the officer of the day into the square, followed next by the brigade band playing the "Dead March." The soldier's arms and legs had been bound before his execution. The regimental chaplain then kneeled with the prisoner in prayer. His comrades, accustomed to the blood and carnage of battlefields, reacted with uncontrollable emotion. The solemn preparation for the execution seemed to be penetrated with the solemnity of the religious services that were conducted.

The needless execution of Johnson served as a public example to federal troops and nearby Confederate forces. The execution of Private Johnson was a tragic event that worsened racial tension in the XXV Corps during that time.

On April 2, 1865, Confederate General Robert E. Lee ordered the evacuation of Richmond by the Confederate government. With the end of open warfare nearing, Confederate soldiers began evacuating Petersburg and Richmond, making their government in the capital city ineffective. When General Lee ordered the evacuation of his soldiers from Petersburg, the Army of Northern Virginia survived a mere seven days before surrendering to General Ulysses Grant at Appomattox Court House, Virginia.

On April 3, 1865, six days before the surrender of the Confederate Army of Northern Virginia at Appomattox, two divisions of the XXV Corps of the Federal Army occupied Richmond. The Confederate government's evacuation and the fall of Richmond led to the emancipation of thousands from enslavement. Upon arrival, the XXV Corps discovered a city engulfed in flames, its citizens unable to quell the fire or the widespread looting. They met no opposition and, upon entering the town, received a hearty welcome from the masses of the people, half of whom were of African descent. Upon the Richmond mayor's surrender, their commanding general, Major General Godfrey Weitzel, entered and took control of the city.

Days after the Confederate government abandoned Richmond, President Abraham Lincoln visited the still-smoldering ruins of the former Confederate Capital. As far as the eye could see, Black and white citizens packed the streets, racing toward Lincoln's vessel. The crowd increased so fast that sailors with fixed bayonets had to withstand the mass of the people. The crowd was eager to shake Mr. Lincoln's hand, touch his coat, or even kneel to kiss his boots.

Patrolling on horseback, Parson observed the crowd around Lincoln grow as he attempted to make his way to the former Confederate White House, now the U.S. military headquarters. Incredibly, only a few sailors were on hand to guard the President against attack. The White House was not far away, but the crowd made movement impossible. Military authorities eventually guided him to the house. It was here he hoped to meet General Weitzel. Instead, Lincoln found a delegation of Southerners waiting to see him to discuss how to bring the war to a speedy, peaceful conclusion.

Witnessing President Lincoln visit the former Confederate capital was the most unforgettable experience of Parson's life. It marked a profound shift in the meaning of his self-liberation perspective, leading to self-discovery and a renewed purpose for his ordeal. Meanwhile, as the Confederate government evacuated Richmond, mobs looted numerous stores, and fires destroyed as many as a thousand buildings.

Following the surrender of the Confederate Army of Northern Virginia and the Confederate government's evacuation, Parson patrolled Richmond's streets. Each patrol step was a muted affirmation, a testament to his unwavering pursuit of self-liberation and the fight for civil and human rights. Lacking a national post-Civil War recovery plan, Parson contemplated that the first steps of stabilization and occupation would be the most difficult. Seated on his horse with his shoulder, hip, and heel perfectly aligned, his brogue boots wedged in the stirrups, Parson rode along the streets as the liberated crowd cheered, bowed, and gave thanks.

Upon taking control of Richmond, the Federal soldiers discovered the city's greatest commodity was neither agricultural produce nor manufactured goods but enslaved Black Americans. To accommodate this lucrative commerce, Richmond offered auction houses, hotels for buyers and sellers, and specialized facilities known as "slave jails" equipped to house the enslaved people. One of the most prominent and most notorious of the Richmond businesses that specialized in buying and selling enslaved Black people was Lumpkin's Jail.

As Parson retold the vignette, in the Shockoe Bottom district of Richmond, the Lumpkin's Jail was a remarkable complex that featured a massive brick retaining wall, which divided the site into upper and lower levels. The kitchen building on the complex served Lumpkin's customers and enslaved people. The site's central courtyard had brick drains that still channeled water below the modern ground surface. The jail building was in the lowest and wettest portion of the site.

USCT soldiers brought a sudden and dramatic end to Lumpkin's interstate slave-trading business. On the night of April 2, Lumpkin attempted to board the last departing train with a recently acquired shipment of enslaved people. Turned away by armed guards, Lumpkin marched the group back to the jail and locked them up for what would be their last night of captivity. When the Federal forces entered the city the following day, an exuberant crowd of Black Americans gathered on Broad Street near Lumpkin's Jail. As Federal soldiers opened the jail, they found and freed the grateful enslaved people who tearfully thanked God and "Master Abe."

Following the fall of Richmond, formerly enslaved people re-purposed Robert Lumpkin's Jail as centers for public worship and education. Lumpkin's notorious brick enslavement jail became the home of a Black seminary that is now known as Virginia Union University, a historically Black university. The pure joy and relief of freedom showed in loud shouts and tears of deep emotion, a sharp contrast to the thin faces and hunched shoulders that were the physical toll of enslavement.

For the jail to become a center of Black education was an extraordinary development since the former Confederate states had prohibited teaching enslaved people how to read and write. The burning desire to learn now shone brightly in the eyes of the newly liberated people, a hunger for knowledge that fueled their minds and straightened their backs.

In 1865, Parson hoped that the Federal victory would ultimately end enslavement. From his insight into enslavement and military experiences, Parson acquired some crucial life lessons for future conflicts, highlighting his intuition and advocacy for the employment, education, and political empowerment of Black people in Southampton County. However, the suspension of open hostilities developed into a turbulent and transitional period.

Although Parson considered the Emancipation Proclamation a monumental step forward. However, he also believed it did not go far enough in guaranteeing true freedom and opportunity for formerly enslaved people. Nevertheless, he argued that it primarily addressed enslaved people in former Confederate states, leaving many unprotected and failing to provide a guaranteed framework for economic and social integration after liberation.

It allowed Parson to join the Federal Army, enabling him to pursue his journey of self-liberation and become an advocate for freedom. Parson dedicated himself to the pursuit of true equality, putting considerable consideration, deliberation, and attention into it. He envisioned a more comprehensive approach that would include land redistribution, access to education, and legal protections to ensure Black citizens could fully participate in American society and escape the lingering effects of enslavement.

This significant proclamation specifically targeted the states that had seceded from the Union while intentionally preserving enslavement in the loyal border states. His vision centered on advocating for policies that went beyond just legal freedom to tackle the systemic inequalities still affecting the entire nation. Ending enslavement became a lasting fight for freedom and liberty after the surrender of the former Confederate states. The proclamation was a promise of freedom and liberty for all citizens.

The proclamation granted independence to the Black people enslaved on Jacob Williams' plantation, among them Parson. However, eighty-four-year-old Jacob showed no inclination to change. He seemed incapable of envisioning a society in which Black people had equality, justice, and citizenship. His steadfast refusal to yield to the enslavement of others was driven by something beyond economic gain, but also hatred, revenge, and racism.

As Parson learned that the proclamation added a moral objective to the reason and cause of the war, strengthening it both militarily and politically. To Parson, emancipation was a promise of full citizenship for formerly enslaved Black people. Following two more years of war, the emancipation in the seceded states, and the Confederate defeat, Lincoln was still unprepared to fulfill promises of education, landownership, and political participation.

On April 15, 1865, during a morning roll call at Fort Burnham, he learned that someone had shot Lincoln, and he died early that morning. Vice President Andrew Johnson became President after the assassination of Abraham Lincoln. While Parson always expected to face hostility from local white citizens, now he must contend with a commander-in-chief whose commitment to protecting formerly enslaved people was waning. After the Presidency fell upon Andrew Johnson, an old-fashioned southern Jacksonian Democrat and enslaver, he never implemented Lincoln's conceptual Ten-Percent Plan.

Following his experience in combat, Parson faced significant challenges, including a shift in his identity, the potential for increased social status because of his military service, and the experiences he acquired during the war. For the rest of his three-year enlistment agreement, he prepared to reintegrate into civilian life, specifically with the social benefits he enjoyed because of emancipation.

As the Civil War was ending, the country had to create a crucial and urgent plan to deal with emancipation, rebuilding, and its initial post-war phase. The collaboration between the Radical Republicans and formerly enslaved Black people, and the emancipation and recruitment of Black regiments, all shaped the formation of the era. Institutional racism and social structures actively worked to suppress the rights of Black people in the nation and maintain a racially segregated society.

For Parson, reconstructing, integrating, and readmitting the Confederate states to the Union was going to be a challenge. Throughout the Federal Army, commanders prepared for Reconstruction and stability operations. In Parson's view, however, the key ingredients of Reconstruction were the fundamental principles of justice, full citizenship rights for all, and genuine equality before the law. Without each of these three elements, he will never reach total self-liberation.

His insights revealed a sense of uncertainty among white individuals regarding how to interact with Black people. This uncertainty arose following the suspension of regular warfare and the subsequent end of enslavement. It became evident that the aim of integrating formerly enslaved individuals into society as free citizens with equal rights did not align with the anticipated outcomes. In Southampton County, Parson found persistent, racial hatred against Black troops, formerly enslaved people, and those who aided them.

CHAPTER ONE

Bureau of Negro Affairs

Dawn cracked open over southeastern Virginia, and with it, everything seemed to stir. Slumbering wild cherry trees dotted the horizon, their branches stretching out—almost as if they knew something was about to change. The land was quiet, but you could almost feel it holding its breath. At Fort Burnham, the air was thick with that same sense of waiting. That skyline—usually so still—was about to wake to the call of Reveille, the bugle's sharp notes cutting through the hush, summoning the United States Colored Troops. For Parson and his brothers, the morning was not just a start; it was a summons to a new adventure.

Back in November 1863, Major General Benjamin Butler returned to the Department of Virginia and North Carolina for the second time. Just a few weeks later, he signed General Order No. 46, and with it, the Office of Superintendent of Negro Affairs was born. Suddenly, there was a mission—to protect, to teach, to care for the people who had been waiting, scattered and uncertain, all 80,000 of them. Butler found them everywhere, and he did not want their futures to be tied to the military's needs. He made it plain: the lives and futures of Black men and women deserved real attention. He wanted labor policies that matched the humanitarian push from Northern missionaries, not just Army priorities. It was not officially called Reconstruction yet, but the Office of Negro Affairs was already doing that work—civil affairs, relief, a lifeline in a place still bracing for more war.

By 1864, Parson saw firsthand how much the Office mattered. Black families and soldiers who had gotten to the Federal side were looking to help establish a life than they had previously experienced. The Office looked after them found them work, set up schools, and kept families together. After his enlistment in December 1864, Parson learned the Army was divided by geography, with Departments like fiefdoms reporting up to the War Department. His own ordeal started under General Butler's watch. The Office of Negro Affairs, Butler's idea, wasn't just shuffling papers. It was writing new rules for life after slavery, sketching out how to help whole communities survive and change.

Even as war raged, the Office started laying the groundwork for something like peace—reconciliation, rebuilding, a new economy. Its work in civil affairs and humanitarian relief helped the Army keep order and start healing the region. They had to put down uprisings, fend off resistance, and push back against the violence of the old order. They made Black settlements on land that used to belong to Confederates, turning what had been symbols of power into places of hope.

The government started planning for life after enslavement even before they had figured out what "emancipation" would really mean. Lincoln's worry was always stability—could he trust the old Southern states to come back into the fold? Even in 1862, after Nashville fell, Lincoln was already hoping to build loyal governments in the South. But nothing came easy. The field commanders—the men actually in charge—had their own ideas. If they did not believe in the mission, it did not happen. Old hatreds and racism, both personal and institutional, colored everything. The mission's goals got muddy, and that confusion trickled down into bad plans, poor prep, and never enough resources to match the need.

Before Parson escaped Jacob Williams' farm, he watched the war between humanity and inhumanity play out up close. Slavery was a monster, infecting politics, society, the economy. From the earliest days of the war, Parson saw people like himself resist, fight, and dream of something freer.

From December 1864 to November 1867, Parson watched the government's post-war occupation unfold. He understood, painfully, just how little agreement existed in Washington about what should come next. The President and Congress were never quite on the same page. Orders to the men in the field were confusing or contradictory. For newly freed Black citizens, the years after the war were dangerous—a time of violence, legal traps, and social rejection. The old beliefs, the ones that said Black people should know their place, didn't just disappear with the end of slavery. Black families had to fight on every front—against the law, against their neighbors, against the weight of history.

Every morning, as Parson lined up for Reveille, the memories of war hung heavy—too many dead, too much horror. The end of open fighting did not mean they were done. The victors, men like Parson, were now supposed to help rebuild. But the wounds were raw, and the memories too close. As he stood at attention, he wondered how Lincoln could bring the country back together—how he could welcome the old enemy back and still protect the rights of the newly freed.

With open war suspended and Reconstruction underway, Parson took up the cause in his own quiet way, pushing for freedom everywhere he could. Self-liberation was never just about him, it was about everyone, about sharing in the victory, about building something lasting. He understood Lincoln's goal: to knit the country together again, but not at the expense of Black rights. Parson's focus was clear, to help steer the country away from the old poisons of prejudice. He read every circular, every bulletin, searching for signs of real progress.

At Fort Burnham, the days fell into a rhythm. There was safety, at least, and plenty of time to drill—sometimes for war, sometimes for the work of peace. Stable duty, sentry posts, and chores filled the days. In the evenings, Parson and his brothers Joseph and Henry taught themselves to read and write, swapping letters and stories, learning from each other whenever they could. Baseball, horseshoes, talk somehow, during uncertainty, these things became lifelines. The end of open war meant Parson could read newspapers, magazines, pamphlets—anything he could get his hands on, and he did so hungrily, relishing freedom that was still new.

White officers in the Office of Negro Affairs took on the work of teaching Black soldiers to read and write—the very skills that slavery had denied them. Schoolhouses, run by churches or Northern missionaries, popped up in Richmond. But even learning had its dangers; Parson saw violence firsthand: teachers and students pelted with rocks, schools set on fire, gunshots in the night. It was never easy, never safe.

Even with the war over, Parson kept watch at night, wary of Confederate sympathizers bent on making trouble. He and his brothers talked often about lost family—mothers, fathers, wives, and children scattered by slavery and war. For so many, the highest hope was simply to find each other again. Some soldiers posted ads in newspapers or wrote letters, desperate for news, working with the Office of Negro Affairs to reconnect with loved ones.

But news from home in Southampton County came rarely. Parson knew the Emancipation Proclamation had not ended slavery everywhere, but it changed everything for millions. Seeing its effects, he learned what emancipation meant, not just as an idea, but as a life-altering reality.

The war had emptied the fields back home. Jacob Williams, the man Parson had escaped, barely had time to plant. There was work to be done, and Parson longed to be there— wanted to help his family through the chaos, wanted to stand before Frances in his blue uniform and tell her all the things he had never been able to say.

Learning to advocate for himself and others became Parson's new calling. Information was power, and with it, he found the courage to push for full emancipation. The war was not just about putting the country back together—it was a fight for what was right. Parson fought for justice, for equality, for the chance at citizenship that he and so many others deserved.

When he enlisted in 1864, Parson remembered, Butler treated Black soldiers as equals. He protected their rights, encouraged them to fight for the Union, and believed that service could build independence and self-reliance—qualities that slavery had tried to crush. Butler's superintendents—C. B. Wilder, Orlando Brown, and Horace James took up the work of creating new settlements, making communities out of chaos. They tried to balance the missionaries' care with the Army's pragmatism, hoping, maybe, to change the status quo just enough to make real freedom possible. But prejudice ran deep, and their efforts met constant resistance.

The news that Butler had been relieved of command, as stated in War Department Order 1 on January 8, 1865, hit Parson hard. Butler's Office of Negro Affairs had set the blueprint for what would come next, for all the government's later post-war plans. Those early acts of civil relief and stabilization helped the Army keep the peace, at least for a little while.

April 3, 1865. The Confederate Army ran from Richmond, and humanitarian aid became the government's priority. Rich or poor, everyone was desperate—starving, ragged, hollow-eyed. The war had devoured livestock, burned barns, and wrecked machines. Recovery would be slow, painful, and expensive. General Weitzel drew on his experience from previous occupations, shifting his men from fighters to caretakers overnight. The Black troops of the XXV Corps moved into Jefferson Davis's old mansion, while the provost marshal took over C Street.

In the city square, USCT soldiers stacked their rifles and formed bucket brigades, racing to douse fires and restore order. Richmond was a ruin—fields empty, people hungry, the old order shattered. Thousands were displaced, and what government remained was almost nothing. That first night, Parson watched his brothers put out flames, protect the city, make it safe for something new to take root.

The Office of Negro Affairs took charge of food distribution, carving Richmond into thirty districts, each run by a pair of civilians, most with experience in charity work. Hunger was not solved overnight, but tragedy was held at bay. And then there was farming—fields needed planting, but time was running out. The labor system had to be rebuilt from scratch.

Now the formerly enslaved were free, and nobody could force them back to the fields. The Office became a kind of employment agency, trying to find a balance: get the crops in, but make sure the workers were paid and treated as men and women, not property. Food rations for the able-bodied depended on willingness to work, but the Army kept a close watch on the landowners, demanding fair pay and fair treatment.

Still, some things made Parson's blood run cold. There were men—traitors in their hearts—now holding government positions, doling out rations to Black people who had to swallow their pride just to survive. Sometimes these men used their power to hurt, to humiliate. The Office of Negro Affairs did what it could, handing out support and resources, trying to keep hope alive.

History's sweep was all around, but for Parson, it was personal: a story written in sweat, fear, hope, and the slow, stubborn push toward something better.

On April 6, 1865, the 114th USCT Infantry Regiment marched triumphantly through Petersburg. This occurred after the capture of Richmond and the surrender of the Confederate Army of Northern Virginia. It was a significant victory for the Federal army during the Civil War, and the city saw a display of the nation's military might. This triumphant march was significant due to the large number of Black soldiers involved in the XXV Corps, who played a crucial role in capturing Petersburg.

As the XXV Corps lined up its divisions along Main Street, the heroes enjoyed a view of the city's central area as they passed. The scene was one of congratulations to the loyalists, but it evoked different feelings among the dissenting citizens. The spectacle was impressive, and the marching was excellent, just as Parson would have anticipated. The men all looked healthy, but some regiments showed unmistakable signs of exhaustion.

The patrols carried out their civil-military duties effectively, and the citizens experienced a level of safety concerning themselves and their property that they had not known in Confederate times. All citizens were required to be in their houses by ten o'clock unless they had the proper pass from the authorities allowing them to stay out later. The city was remarkably peaceful, even more so than at any point during the rebellion.

The egress after the victory march posed several difficulties. Black soldiers in blue uniforms, standing prepared, repeatedly stopped citizens and ordered them to halt. After a few questions, sentries told them to move on. If their credentials were satisfactory after inspection, they could continue until they were stopped by the next sentry about a block away. The same procedure was repeated at each stop, which was confusing to civilians but necessary for the city's security.

In May 1865, the Federal Army celebrated its victory with the Grand Review of the Armies. Specifically, the Army of the Potomac, the Army of the Cumberland, and the Army of Tennessee all paraded through Washington, D.C., the nation's capital. The polished appearance of these troops reflected their excellent discipline. There, they received praise from the crowds and reviews from politicians, officials, and prominent citizens for preserving the Union and ending enslavement. Conspicuously missing were the 175 USCT regiments, which made up one-tenth of the Federal Army and played a vital role in securing victory.

In April 1865, Parson was on sentry duty at City Point when he met and spoke with Sergeant Richard Etheridge. Etheridge was the Sergeant of the Guard and a member of the 36th Infantry USCT Regiment. As they patrolled the streets, a deep, abiding sense of purpose settled over him, fueling his growing desire to obtain full freedom.

They discussed the conflict in Texas, weighing the reasons for and against engaging in battles beyond his struggles. Parson felt the conflict was a stark contrast to the present fight for human and civil rights in his homeland. Inspired by Sergeant Etheridge, he came to understand that their experience as part of the USCT was connected to a broader movement of emancipation.

Parson read after-action reports about the conflict and the battles occurring along the Texas-Mexico border. Soon, he realized he needed to be mentally and physically prepared for deployment to the Rio Grande east of Brownsville, Texas. Parson's deep understanding of and empathy for Mexicans' suffering helped him let go of his fixed ideas about the past, allowing him to stay curious and open-minded.

Unsurprisingly, the lack of written instructions often led to misinterpretations of military directives, orders, and alerts. This confusion fueled rumors among the USCT soldiers about the battles taking place in Texas and their deployment to Brownsville.

Initially, Parson resisted the call to deploy to Texas. Sergeant Etheridge reached out to him, stating that the Mexicans had to defend themselves against the French. Etheridge said, "In war and peace, it is always good to have allies and friendly neighbors." He explained to Parson the importance of forming helpful alliances, both in Texas and at home, with the Office of Negro Affairs. Deployment to Texas would pull him out of Virginia and lead him toward an international situation that changed his life.

Etheridge informed Parson that while on patrol and ensuring the safety of Richmond's newly freed population, preserving the Union and ending enslavement hung in the balance. However, disobeying military deployment orders was not an option. Etheridge, representing a calm yet authoritative presence, ignited his tendency to advocate for the advancement of civil and human rights. He said he participated in the Federal raid of northeastern North Carolina and witnessed inhumane attacks against enslaved Black people. Sergeant Etheridge warned Parson about publicly sanctioned violent attacks against Black men and women throughout the former Confederacy. These attacks sometimes led to, or culminated in, lynchings and massacres.

Etheridge told Parson that their time in the Army was like formerly enslaved people striving for freedom in refugee camps. In pursuit of his vision of liberty, Parson embraced the challenges. Etheridge told Parson that he also served as an advocate and leader in the civil rights movement during the war for members of the 36th Infantry USCT Regiment.

In a documented case, Sergeant Etheridge said he petitioned the Office of Negro Affairs Assistant Commissioner on behalf of the men in his regiment. In the petition, Etheridge wrote that the Federal government had promised rations for the soldiers' families upon enlistment. However, the assistant superintendent of Negro Affairs stole and sold the rations, leaving the families starving. He grieved that soldiers' families had no protection, while the assistant superintendent was there to protect them and would not do it. For the soldiers of the 36th

Infantry USCT Regiment with family on Roanoke Island, Etheridge humbly petitioned the Assistant Commissioner to favor them by removing the assistant superintendent.

At the end of their sentry duty, Parson asked Etheridge for his insights into the post-war plan and what to expect. He paused, then quickly theorized from his experience as a USCT soldier that the era would begin after the Confederate forces surrendered. During this time, the President would establish and implement guidelines for a swift and lenient post-war process. However, he would face strong opposition from abolitionists and Radical Republicans in Congress.

Next, he warned Parson to expect a period of post-war planning directed from the nation's capital. It would feature a short duration of direct military rule in the seceded states and be challenged by their former politicians and enslavers. The planning would continue in each Confederate state until Congress readmitted that state to the Union. During this time, freed Black people, abolitionists, and Radical Republicans in Congress will seek and gain full citizenship, voting rights, and emancipation in all states and territories.

Finally, Etheridge suggested that the time for loyal Republican governments would arrive. Although short, it would last from the moment civil authorities regained power until the Army's final withdrawal from its occupation role in the former Confederate states. Once a state rejoined the Union, civil authority would take precedence, and military commanders would have no right to intervene except under circumstances that existed before the insurrection. He said, "In war, the victory is just the blossom, and nothing is more frustrating than a bloom that refuses to morph into some fruit."

He amazed Parson with his insight and theory on the post-war plan. As sentry duty ended, Etheridge informed Parson of the Homestead Act, which provided that any adult citizen could claim 160 acres of surveyed government land to form a farm. He believed that advancing civil and human rights was his duty to the country. He saw it as an opportunity to build a new life for himself and others.

Parson, after serving alongside Etheridge, always remembered his theory regarding the post-war plan and imitated his visionary thinking approach. The chance to advance civil and human rights ignited a flame of determination in Parson. His transformation exemplified the experience of many other formerly enslaved people. He discovered reasons for accepting the challenges in the role of an occupier, protecting the newly freed people, and helping allies and friendly neighbors pursue their visions of freedom.

The Homestead Act, enacted during the Civil War in 1862, provided a path for people like Parson to own land for farming. According to the act, after five years on the land, he was entitled to the property, free and clear, except for a small registration fee. He could also acquire the title after only a six-month residency and minor improvements, provided he paid the government $1.25 per acre. The act, however, proved to be no cure-all for poverty. Comparatively few formerly enslaved laborers and farmers could afford to establish a farm or buy the necessary tools, seeds, and livestock.

Over the years, Congress passed new laws to provide more benefits to veterans applying for a homestead. On April 4, 1872, Congress passed an amendment to the law. It gave every service member who served the United States during the Civil War at least 90 days' eligibility to claim up to 160 acres of homestead land. Additionally, veterans could count their military service toward the residency requirement, lowering it to a minimum of one year. The act also allowed these benefits to be transferred to a widow or children. If a soldier died during his enlistment, his entire enlistment period was subtracted from the residency requirement.

After the Civil War, Parson learned that out of the five hundred million acres of government land between 1862 and 1904, only eighty million acres went to homesteaders. Most people who bought land under the act came from nearby areas. Unfortunately, Congress wrote the act so unclearly that it encouraged fraud, and early changes only made it worse. Speculators, cattle owners, miners, loggers, and railroads acquired the land.

Late in April 1865, Parson and his brothers anxiously awaited the anticipated redeployment orders. These orders, they believed, would send them to Texas. The Confederate Army west of the Mississippi River surrendered to Federal officials. Preparing for civil-military duty along the Rio Grande, the XXV Corps spent the rest of April drilling and training to discourage resurgent Confederate activity and guarding the border with Mexico.

After the evacuation of the Confederate government and the fall of Richmond, resistance in the former Confederacy persisted in Texas. On May 18, 1865, after a brief stint of civil-military duty around Richmond, the XXV Corps received the following deployment orders to Texas.

Washington, May 18th, 1865, 12.40 pm.
Major-General H. W. Halleck, Richmond, Va.

Please direct Major-General Weitzel, commanding the XXV Army Corps, to get his corps in readiness for embarkation at City Point immediately upon the arrival of ocean transportation. He will take with him forty days' rations for twenty thousand men, one-half of his land transportation, and one-fourth of his mules with the requisite amount of forage for his animals. All surplus transportation and other public property he may have, he will turn over to the depots at City Point.

By command of

Lieutenant-General Grant.
Signed, John A. Rawlins,
Brigadier-General and Chief of Staff.

While in Richmond, Parson read an after-action report about the final Civil War battle. It occurred when the 62nd Infantry Regiment, USCT, fought against Confederates at Palmito Ranch, Texas. On May 12 and 13, 1865, the 62nd Infantry Regiment, a legendary unit, fought in what would be the last battle of the Civil War. Their efforts on and off the battlefield serve as a historic example of the fight for freedom and equality.

After the war, the USCT soldiers of the 62nd Infantry Regiment played a key role in establishing Lincoln University in Jefferson City, Missouri.

As described in the after-action report, after marching all night, a detachment of the 62nd Infantry Regiment reached the outskirts of the White Ranch. After securing the area, the Federal detachment continued toward Palmito Ranch. Once in view of Palmito Ranch, they encountered a 100-man Texas Cavalry company. After attempting to conceal themselves just beyond the ranch, the Confederates spotted the Federal detachment on the Mexican side of the Rio Grande River.

After losing the element of surprise, the Federal detachment set a battle plan. The Federal detachment moved towards the ranch and hit the outnumbered Confederates along the river and at the ranch. After a few hours of fighting, the Confederates pulled back towards Brownsville and requested reinforcements. The 62nd Infantry USCT pursued the Confederates only a mile from the ranch before resting on a small hill.

During the night, the detachment from the 62nd Infantry USCT requested reinforcements. Early the next morning, the Federal detachment was on the field with two hundred men from the 34th Indiana Infantry Regiment, bringing the total Federal forces to five hundred.

By early afternoon, Confederate reinforcements arrived with four hundred men, including six cannons, which were deadly on the flat prairie. This gave them a significant advantage over the Federal forces. By evening, the Confederates were in position and began their attack. After hitting both flanks and punching the center of their lines, the Federal forces decided to withdraw to Brazos Island. The Confederates continued to pound Federal lines, nearly capturing their entire command. However, the 62nd Regiment USCT stopped them by holding the Federal right flank and keeping the escape route open.

As read by Parson, the Federal forces withdrew a few miles from Palmito Ranch along a bend near the river. Concurrently, the Confederate forces continued to hammer their lines with artillery. The Federal troops finally retreated, ending the last battle of the Civil War. Following the final regular battle in Texas, the Confederate Army west of the Mississippi surrendered to Federal officials.

Later in 1866, veterans of the legendary 62nd Infantry Regiment, USCT, donated a significant portion of their mustering-out pay to help establish Lincoln University for freed Black Americans. This act of collective giving showed their firm commitment to education and to empowering and advancing their community. The soldiers of the 62nd Regiment, whose pay averaged $13 per month, raised $5,000 to create an educational institution in Jefferson City, which they named the Lincoln Institute. The 65th Infantry Regiment, USCT, contributed another $1,400 to the school's endowment.

Upon returning home, the regiment's veterans, who learned to read and write during basic training, were eager to establish a school for other freed Black people. Their legacy remains a testament to the transformative power of education and the enduring spirit of those soldiers who fought for freedom and equality.

Initially, Parson and other USCT soldiers instinctively opposed the news of deployment to Texas and guarding the border with Mexico. Parson felt the gnawing anxiety of such a long journey from Virginia to the distant, unknown expanse of Texas. Convinced that Black regiments were ill-suited to guard the conquered eastern Virginia, Major General Halleck ordered their deployment to Texas.

On May 29, 1865, President Andrew Johnson issued an amnesty proclamation to "induce all persons to return to their loyalty" to the United States of America. After completing his sentry duty at City Point, Parson learned of President Johnson's Proclamation of Amnesty and Reconstruction. It granted amnesty to most former Confederate soldiers and officials, allowing them to regain their property rights if they took an oath of allegiance to the United States. This was the third such Proclamation, but the first to offer amnesty. Johnson extended the oath to all participants in the rebellion.

President Johnson renewed the offer in this Proclamation after the failure of persons connected with the former Confederacy to fulfill the terms by which Lincoln had granted amnesty. The Proclamation insists that people desiring amnesty take an oath to disclaim enslavement and defend the U.S. Constitution. It also exempts certain parties from being eligible for the benefits offered.

President Johnson proclaimed a full, unconditional pardon to all individuals who, directly or indirectly, participated in the recent insurrection or rebellion. He granted amnesty for acts of treason against the United States and for siding with its enemies during the recent Civil War. He restored all rights, privileges, and immunities granted by the Constitution and its laws. The Proclamation excluded high-ranking Confederate leaders from the pardon and required them to apply individually for forgiveness.

The amnesty, stabilization, and occupation were significant steps towards the end of the Civil War and the beginning of the Reconstruction era. It demonstrated Lincoln's vision for a unified nation and his willingness to offer a path back to the Union for those who had fought against it. In contrast, those who had fought against it in other earlier insurrections or rebellions received severe punishment to preempt future conflicts.

As Parson described the Proclamation, it was too lenient for the tough daily life he served in the army, suppressing the rebellion. He worried that the plan did not adequately address the issues of enslavement and racial inequality, potentially allowing for the return of the planter aristocracy and systemic oppression of newly freed people.

The Proclamation represented a moderate approach to reintegration of the former Confederate states, prioritizing a swift return to the Union over more punitive measures. Despite its national healing goals, leniency toward former Confederates and the risk of continued racial inequality sparked significant debate, adding to the post-enslavement and secession difficulties. Federal authorities paroled many Confederate soldiers and officials after the war. Only a few faced executions for treason or war crimes, and authorities either dropped or did not proceed to trial these cases.

As he grew, Parson saw military service as part of his liberation, citizenship, and equality. Through martial skill, he aimed to show the skeptical, prejudiced white majority that they deserved inclusion in the American polity as free and equal citizens. Few white soldiers fought in the Federal Army to end enslavement. Instead, they encouraged young men to volunteer and fight to keep the Union that their grandfathers had helped to create. Saving the Union was their primary goal.

During the Civil War, Parson met soldiers who had many reasons for fighting. Some saw it as a duty to their country, while others viewed it as a chance for adventure or to start a new life. Still, others fought because of the military draft, or conscription, in the loyal states in 1863. Using conscription gave the Federal Army a significant edge over its Confederate opponents.

Parson's trek answered the bold call of military service to pursue his vision of freedom. His self-liberation odyssey showed that formerly enslaved men did not become free just by wearing uniforms or signing enlistment papers. Instead, they experienced emancipation as the first step in a longer process. The men spent their time in the Federal Army as freed people living out, or trying to live out, their visions of freedom, as freed people did in other parts of the war zone.

Eventually, he realized that formerly enslaved men did not find freedom just by wearing uniforms or signing enlistment papers. They had many reasons for accepting the challenges of being an occupier, protecting the newly freed people, and helping to unite the nation. The chance to fight for humanity ignited a fire in Parson, and the USCT regiments, with their determination and battle cries, became feared units in the seceded states.

At the end of open hostilities, Parson proudly embraced Black heritage and promised to advocate for complete emancipation. He discovered the profound significance and relevance of earning freedom, citizenship, and equality for all Black people, not just a retooled version of the status quo ante. Parson began to transform himself and his vision of human and civil rights. This change promoted a vision of how he would continue his self-liberation through changes in economic growth, social development, agricultural modernization, and political reconciliation.

With thirty-three months remaining on his enlistment, Parson's goals were straightforward: survive until he could complete his service honorably and return home. That so many did not was a tragic chapter in American history.

At the suspension of open hostility, residents of the loyal Federal states and those of the former Confederacy debated the role that enslavement played in American society. When open war ended and Reconstruction began, Parson recognized the need for complete emancipation. He supported the rights of both formerly enslaved and freed Black people. He believed that advancing civil and human rights was his duty to the country. He saw it as an opportunity to forge a new life for himself.

The Federal Army's occupation of the former Confederate states was inherently a civil-military operation in scope. It required that the military undertake what officers in the late twentieth century called nation-building. Like nation-building, stabilization occupation encompassed operations to establish or maintain peace, order, and government authority in the hostile former Confederate states. The occupation had two main features, including military operations against irregular forces and civil humanitarian operations for refugees.

As post-war planning advanced, new challenges arose. Due to laws known as the Black Codes, the former Confederate states continued racial inequalities and maintained the oppression of Black people. Debates, both political and moral, centered on the amount and length of support given. For many succeeding years, fierce disputes centered on reconciliation terms, weighing the desire for punishment against the need for rehabilitation.

CHAPTER TWO

Freedmen's Bureau Act

In spring 1865, the effort to reintegrate the states from the defeated Confederacy and the formerly enslaved people into the nation was in a turbulent political climate. From situation reports at Fort Burnham, Parson learned that Congress passed an Act to establish a Bureau for the Relief of Freedmen and Refugees on March 3, 1865. Known as the Freedmen's Bureau, the agency aimed to facilitate the transition from enslavement to freedom and citizenship for Black Americans in the former Confederate states. Before the Freedmen's Bureau, there was no federal policy for civil-military operations at the national level. With the creation of the Bureau, the way forward was clear.

The agency encouraged formerly enslaved people to return to the farms they had previously worked. It had to ensure that the landowners paid these returning workers appropriately and treated them as the formerly enslaved people they now were. To further boost the systems, the Army disbursed abandoned, captured, and excess government horses and mules to formerly enslaved workers. The 1865 crops yielded better-than-expected results, averting famine.

Because of President Johnson's leniency, many former Confederate states successfully enacted legislation to circumscribe Black freedom. They designed these laws to restrict freed Black people's activities and to ensure their availability as a labor force. These repressive laws enraged Parson and consequently added to his anxiety, stress, and lack of fulfillment. By engaging with a mentor, Parson hoped to gain insights, strategies, and emotional support to navigate this significant life transition. He recognized the importance of seeking guidance and support from a mentor to help him navigate the challenges of emancipation.

Parson, along with his brothers Joseph and Henry, had not seen their parents since their daring escape from enslavement on Jacob Williams' farm in December 1864. The chaos and tensions that existed in Virginia following the Civil War alarmed Parson, leading to his descent into self-doubt and loss of confidence. Formerly enslaved men began seeking voting rights, forming political parties, owning agricultural land, and assuming control of labor in many areas. However, the most immediate task, with long-term implications, was attending to agribusiness obligations.

Under a sky heavy with simmering tension, Parson and his brothers patrolled the dusty Richmond roads. During the occupation of Richmond, their thoughts and discussions drifted to hostilities in Southampton County and the progress of humanitarian relief efforts. They also wondered about Solomon and Louisa, hoping they were managing well with their newly found freedom. A nagging question lingered in their conscience about whether Jacob held them responsible for their sons' self-emancipation.

As the Army established the national-level civil-military operations doctrine, the War Department began the demobilization of federal forces and their transfer to discharge camps back home. During the suspension of open war hostilities, Parson soon discovered that USCT regiments made up about one-third of the federal forces occupying former Confederate states. Dispatched throughout Richmond, Black troops kept order while the Federal government attempted to rebuild the nation.

Their presence in crisp uniforms against the backdrop of still-smoldering ruined buildings was a visual reminder of defeat to the former capital. Because of complaints from white citizens, the War Department took steps to remove most Black units from the city and reassigned in the countryside throughout the state. About three months into the occupation of Richmond, it ordered XXV Corps to plan and prepare for redeployment to the Department of Texas.

At the start of Reconstruction, the widespread defiance, unrest, and strain emanating from the former Confederacy in post-war Virginia profoundly subdued Parson's sense of assurance and self-worth. His emancipation began with a significant character flaw rooted in his enslavement and the inner conflicts that add to his turmoil. The occupation of Richmond by XXV Corps USCT regiments, armed and dressed in a dark blue coat and sky-blue pants, only aggravated tensions.

Virginia's provisional government and local authorities' efforts to reestablish white supremacy and return Black people to conditions like enslavement disturbed Parson. Considering this broader perspective on Parson's life, he had his reasons for his point of view, including a complex mix of personal, social, economic, and political insights. The former Confederate sympathizers, with their hateful glares and muttered curses, temporarily interrupted Parson's focus on freeing himself.

From his point of view, Parson observed two main obstacles that he had to overcome as the operation began. They included military engagements against irregular forces that imposed violent resistance to the Federal army's rule. The civil humanitarian activities included the distribution of food, clothing, and supplies to millions of formerly enslaved people. As he learned, despite facing significant obstacles, the Federal government provided vital aid and support to formerly enslaved people during a critical period of transition.

Before the Freedmen's Bureau, the Federal Army used the system Butler created for the Black settlements in Virginia and North Carolina. He designed and implemented a system for putting Black people on their feet. It also defended them against those who will strive to push them down and keep them down. No other military Department created such a system during the war. As Parson recounted the chaos, he wondered if Butler could have set up such a valuable system across all the former

Confederate states if he had overseen the Army's humanitarian efforts.

The Bureau represented an unprecedented move by the Federal government to address social welfare and labor relations. As Parson continued the journey and grew, however, he gained a deeper understanding of the military rule and occupation of the former Confederate states. Early in the civil-military operation, Parson believed his ongoing struggle for racial equality was nearing a successful completion, only to realize he still had a long way to go.

Late in April 1865, USCT regiments continued to carry out essential civil-military operations. These efforts went beyond traditional combat, involving military actions against irregular Confederate forces and guerrilla groups that persisted in violently resisting Federal authority and the new order. These engagements often included patrolling occupied territories, suppressing insurgent activity, and protecting Black settlements from harassment and violence by former Confederates and other hostile groups.

The USCT's presence served as a symbol of Federal authority and a crucial component in maintaining peace and security during the turbulent start of Reconstruction. After Lincoln's assassination, President Johnson's waning regard for emancipation caused Parson to lose hope. He was at a low point in his self-liberation ordeal, and readmitting the former Confederate states felt like a botched mission. Their violent resistance to emancipation disturbed Parson, leading to an eerie feeling of self-doubt and a loss of confidence.

During the period of military rule and occupation, Henry McNeal Turner, the Chaplain of the 1st Cavalry USCT Regiment, played a crucial role in guiding USCT soldiers. He helped them overcome their initial anxieties and prepare for deployment to Mexico. When military operations were less active, Chaplain Turner endeavored to conduct at least one prayer service each week, preferably on Sunday. Parson recognized Chaplain Turner as a knowledgeable and experienced individual with whom he had already formed a professional relationship. Between prayer meetings, Turner provided Black soldiers with the knowledge and information to succeed in the Army.

Turner, as an army chaplain, dodged musket bullets and cannon grapeshot, comforted the sick and wounded, and settled disputes between white Southerners and their former enslaved workers. Turner led prayer meetings, cared for and prayed with the wounded warriors, and saw that soldiers' pay reached their families. He also wrote letters for those who could not write. He functioned as an intermediary between the Black troops and white commanding officers. More importantly, Turner taught the men in the regiment how to read.

After prayer meetings, Parson and his brothers often met with Turner when he was available to assist the soldiers in resolving their most significant human and civil rights issues. Parson witnessed Turner's debates regarding emancipation and the enlistment of Black people as Federal troops.

Turner informed the brothers that he was the first of fourteen Black chaplains to serve in the Federal Army during the war. Born free in 1833, his mother and maternal grandmother raised and guided him with faith in their capabilities and those of Black people. Because it was illegal to teach Black people, he taught himself to read and write in South Carolina. Like Parson, Turner advocated for the establishment of churches and schools for the formerly enslaved people, who had been barred from attending either.

As the Civil War neared its victorious conclusion, the nation needed civil and human rights measures to integrate the formerly enslaved Black people into society. As Parson observed, their daily life was a relentless struggle for survival, marked by violence from racism. Emancipation did not ease their deplorable condition. The formerly enslaved Black people remained poorly fed, clothed, and uneducated. Eventually, Parson learned that Reconstruction would not be a single event, but an ongoing process shaped by the shared visions of freedom held by Black women and men, Congressional representatives, and the President.

Turner evinced his firm belief in the absolute equality of Black people with whites and insisted on civil rights for all Black citizens. Parson respected his clear or deep perception of the formerly enslaved people's situation and reached out to Chaplain Turner after a prayer meeting at Fort Burnham. He asked Turner to give him advice, wisdom, information, or insight that would prepare him for the voyage ahead. They agreed to meet and talk during their breaks from duty. They met and discussed human and civil rights. Parson sought his help and insight by mail when they were unable to meet in person.

When Parson and his brothers met with Chaplain Turner, he informed them that ex-Confederate officers had formed the Ku Klux Klan (KKK) in 1865. According to Turner, it was an insurgent vehicle for white southern resistance to the federal policies aimed at establishing political and economic equality for Black people. Its members extended into every former Confederate state. They waged underground excursions of intimidation and violence directed at white Republican leaders and Black people.

With the indistinct murmur of Chaplain Turner's voice, Parson gained confidence, insight, and advice to overcome his initial fears and confront the complex mix of human and civil rights issues. Turner's wisdom, like the fleeting beauty of cherry blossoms, guided how to conquer anxieties and motivated Parson to confront the current moment. When a change came over other Black troops, and they became sullen and undisciplined, Parson used the lessons that Turner taught him.

During a meeting with the soldiers, Chaplain Turner told them about the Bureau that Congress had created. As he explained, it provided food, shelter, clothing, medical services, and land to displaced refugees, including newly freed Black Americans. The Bureau was meant to operate during the Civil War and for one year afterward. It established schools, oversaw contracts between formerly enslaved people and employers, and managed confiscated or abandoned lands.

Turner said the Bureau's mission was to provide relief and help formerly enslaved people become self-sufficient. Its functions included issuing rations and clothing, operating hospitals and refugee camps, and supervising labor contracts between planters and newly freed people. It served as a federal agency to direct provisions, clothing, and fuel for the immediate and temporary shelter. It also supplied federal aid to destitute and suffering refugees, formerly enslaved people, and their wives and children. The Bureau's early activities included supervising abandoned and confiscated property.

The Bureau also handled apprenticeships, conflicts, and grievances, and assisted benevolent societies in creating schools. It helped legalize marriages entered during enslavement. It provided transportation to refugees and freed people who were attempting to reunite with their families or move to other parts of the country. Congress created the Bureau partly to redistribute confiscated land from the former Confederacy. It gave legal title for 40-acre plots to Black people and white Federal loyalists.

Congress established the Bureau just over a month before John Wilkes Booth assassinated President Lincoln. When Andrew Johnson became President, he often clashed with Radical Republicans in Congress over the Bureau's handling of relief and help for formerly enslaved people.

Rumors continued to spread among the 1st Cavalry Regiment, USCT, claiming they were ordered to Texas to pick cotton to help cover war expenses. Deployment to Texas to secure the entire eastern half of an anti-imperialist front made perfect sense to the Army. However, this assignment held little appeal for the many Black soldiers who had enlisted to end enslavement. Initially, the men resisted orders, fearing re-enslavement. Labor duties, including working with cotton, were a reality for many USCT units during the war.

Late in April 1865, as the longer-serving white troops were being discharged, most of the Black soldiers still had at least a year left on their enlistment contracts. After the last Confederate troops laid down their weapons, the USCT regiments of the XXV Corps prepared for redeployment to Texas. The troops heard disturbing rumors despite the announcement of their deployment to the Mexican border. One story was that the Federal government was going to send them south instead, to work on the cotton plantations to pay the national debt.

Officers assured many soldiers who inquired that the rumors about cotton picking were false. Certain XXV Corps regiments were also worried about family safety, shelter, and food. Near Fort Monroe, returning former Confederate landowners were charging the soldiers' families high rents or evicting them as squatters. Soon, a change came over the USCT troops, and they became sullen and undisciplined.

Major General Godfrey Weitzel, the first to help liberate the enslaved people from the capital of the Confederacy, understood the irony of Black Federal soldiers fearing re-enslavement. The rumor that the 1st Cavalry Regiment was sent to Texas to pick cotton to offset war expenses seems to be more speculation and propaganda than a mission. Weitzel empathized with the freemen and formerly enslaved people he led, who showed dedication to the country and a commitment to their freedom.

Using the lessons that Turner taught him, Parson attempted to convince the Black troops to serve loyally, even under the current conditions. He understood that the Federal Navy had acquired the USS Meteor (1863), a gunboat, during the American Civil War. The vessel carried heavy artillery and became part of the sea blockade of the waterways of the breakaway Confederate States of America. As he described, the gunboat's purpose was to transport the men, and some of them took heed. This mutinous spirit intensified, and when the units arrived at Hampton Roads, they boarded the steamship Meteor, which was to transport them to Texas.

On May 18, 1865, the War Department transferred the entire XXV Corps, led by General Weitzel, to Brownsville, Texas, for occupation duty. Knowing Johnson, an old-fashioned southern Democrat and enslaver, the soldiers doubted his commitment to protect formerly enslaved people from re-enslavement. However, a change came over the USCT troops, and they became more hostile and undisciplined. This increased, and when the units got to Hampton Roads, they boarded the steamship Meteor, which was to take them to Texas.

Johnson issued the Amnesty Proclamation on May 29, 1865, effectively renewing Lincoln's offer to pardon Confederates who took a loyalty oath to the Union and accepted the abolition of enslavement. However, it increased the number of classes, except for the benefits of the proclamation, from seven to fourteen. His plan was the same as the one that Lincoln had advocated and attempted to implement. However, when Johnson adopted the same policy, it looked more suspicious.

His amnesty proclamation was more severe than Lincoln's. It disqualified all former Confederate military and civil officers, as well as anyone owning property worth $20,000 or more, making their estates subject to confiscation. The apparent goal was to shift political power in the former Confederate state from the old planter aristocracy to small farmers and artisans. It aimed to bring about a societal revolution.

Within three months after his inauguration, Johnson had set the forces by which he hoped that peace and tranquility might prevail. The Federal government once again became a unified whole. In the execution of the amnesty proclamation, he had not sought the cooperation or advice of Congress. Confident of the correctness of his ideas, feeling sure that they were a correct interpretation of the Constitution, he pursued his policy of leniency.

With Congress in adjournment from April to December 1865, Johnson put his plan into operation. Under provisional governors appointed by him, the former Confederate states held conventions that voided or repealed their ordinances of secession, abolished enslavement, and repudiated Confederate debts. Their newly elected legislatures ratified the constitutional Amendment, which guaranteed freedom for Black Americans. By the end of 1865, every former Confederate state except Texas had reestablished civil government.

At first, President Johnson pleased the Black people and Republican allies by publicly attacking the planter aristocracy and insisting on punishment for the rebellion. After he took office, the only modification of his policy was an increase in clemency for the former Confederates. President Johnson did not let many days pass after his inauguration before he started to show the expected signs of his attitude towards Black people.

The control of whites over Black people, however, resurfaced, as each of the newly elected state legislatures enacted statutes severely limiting the freedom and rights of Black people. They restricted the ability of Black people to own land and to work as free laborers. They denied them most of the civil and political rights enjoyed by whites. Moreover, the disenfranchised Confederate leaders won many of the offices in the new governments. Rather than ordering new elections, Johnson granted pardons on a large scale. He showed little interest in protecting Black civil rights or protecting Black people from violence and intimidation.

Parson believed that Johnson's vision for the nation, and particularly the legal status of formerly enslaved people, clashed with that of many Black people and their Republican allies. He acquiesced to the legislature, which former Confederate governments enacted to reduce formerly enslaved people to the pre-war status of dependent plantation laborers. Johnson vetoed a string of Republican-backed measures, including an extension of the Freedmen's Bureau and the first Civil Rights bill. He ordered Black families evicted from land on which the Federal Army had settled them.

An outraged Northern public believed that Johnson's lenient policy was losing the fruits of victory. His tactics drove the moderates into the radical camp.

On May 30, 1865, President Johnson appointed Major General Oliver Otis Howard as the commissioner of the newly created Freedmen's Bureau. He issued orders to his assistant commissioners, who managed the Bureau's daily operations in the seceded states, Border States, and the District of Columbia.

The Federal government made early efforts to document the marriages of formerly enslaved people. They began with military officers and civilians who supervised contraband camps where formerly enslaved people sought refuge during the Civil War. The Military Department issued marriage licenses and certificates. It instructed chaplains and missionaries on their proper use. The wartime superintendents later transferred many of the Office of Negro Affairs' marriage registers and other marriage records to the Bureau upon its formation.

Howard continued this practice, which the Military Department of Virginia and North Carolina had initiated in the Federal government's refugee camps. He authorized his subordinates to designate officers to keep a record of marriages in places where the local statutes made no provisions for the marriage of persons of color. He authorized the assistant commissioners to keep records of marriages, which any ordained minister of the gospel may solemnize. Howard's orders also required ministers to report on marriages they performed, including "such items as may be required for registration at places designated by assistant commissioners." Marriages that military officers had already recorded were to be preserved.

Commissioner Howard's marriage orders provided necessary guidance for solemnizing enslavement marriages.

However, his instructions and the several ways in which assistant commissioners responded to them led to variations in the data collected about formerly enslaved couples. Due to these variations, the quantity of Bureau marriage records varied by state. For some states, no marriage records were available.

At Fort Burnham, Parson learned that under Howard's marriage orders, it was lawful for him and Frances to get married. It also included having their marriage certificate recorded by the government. As customary, however, Army company commanders advised single soldiers against marrying before completing their enlistment, believing this to be the wisest course.

Parson wanted to know more about the wages of his parents and the other freed workers on Jacob's farm in Southampton County. During his encampment in Texas, he learned that the Freedmen's Bureau supervised labor contracts between planters and freed people.

In June 1865, President Johnson appointed Federal Brevet Brigadier General Orlando Brown as Assistant Commissioner of the Freedmen's Bureau in Virginia. The Bureau's operations in Virginia began that same month when he set up his headquarters in Richmond.

Assistant Commissioner Brown received letters from formerly enslaved people, local white citizens, state officials, and other non-Bureau personnel. These letters varied from complaints to job applications in the Bureau. The Assistant

Commissioner corresponded with both his superior in the Washington Bureau headquarters and his subordinate officers in the subdistricts. Based upon reports submitted to him by the sub-assistant commissioners and other subordinate staff officers, he prepared reports that he sent to the Commissioner concerning Bureau activities in areas under his authority.

Before the suspension of open war hostilities, the Bureau of Negro Affairs in the Military Department of Virginia patrolled Virginia to enforce the Emancipation Proclamation and protect the newly freed people. Many white Virginians expressed outrage at the presence of USCT soldiers in the role of occupiers. They petitioned Provisional Governor Francis Harrison Pierpont to remove the Black soldiers who patrolled at the county level. They felt their presence was repugnant and humiliating to white Virginians' feelings. In addition, they feared the troops would have an improper and injurious influence on the formerly enslaved Black people.

As Parson's journey developed, he viewed the military rule as a plausible path to sustained emancipation. He sought to win over skeptical white society by showcasing the military excellence of Black soldiers and proving their worth as equal citizens. Sergeant Etheridge warned Parson about and described the publicly sanctioned violent attacks against freed Black men and women, sometimes leading to, or culminating in, massacres. From this warning, Parson discovered the challenges he faced and used the advice like an athlete would in practicing with a skilled physical training partner.

Following Lincoln's assassination, formerly enslaved people found themselves lost in a subdued and defeated Virginia. The situation ignited a rebellious spirit within the Regiments of the XXV Corps at Fort Monroe. On June 10, 1865, the 1st Cavalry Regiment, USCT, moved to City Point, Virginia, and then sailed for Texas. The regiment began to come down in two shallow-draft Army steamers: four companies aboard the SS Wilmon Whilldin that afternoon, and eight companies on the SS Delaware the next morning.

The 2nd Cavalry Regiment, USCT, also boarded that morning at City Point. They made threats that they would not "be sent to Texas" and that the government had no right to send them there. The others, who regarded them as grumbling peculiar to the Black race, paid no attention to these grumbles.

The next day, the XXV Corps placed the regiment on a small, light-draft river steamer and sailed down the James River to Hampton Roads. The regiments went aboard the ship hesitantly and began their journey down the river. On June 16, 1865, the regiment sailed from Hampton Roads. The fleet comprised five vessels and steamers, including the General McClellan, Meteor, Ashland, H. S. Hagan, and Dudley Buck. It stopped at Fort Morgan, Alabama, for orders, then proceeded southwest, passing the Mississippi River, to load coal and water.

When the Federal Army then appointed Colonel Jeptha Dudley Garrard to command the 1st Regiment Cavalry, USCT, he understood that the XXV Corps was going to Mexico to intervene against the French. However, the malicious rumors continued to spread among the Black troops. Parson told him that the story was that the government was planning to send them south to work on cotton plantations to pay off the national debt.

He advised Colonel Garrard to dismiss the rumor and assure the Black men that it was untrue. They initially seemed content; however, a noticeable change ensued, marked by sullenness and disobedience. This increased, and when the units got to Hampton Roads, they boarded the steamship Meteor, which was to take them to Texas. Parson knew the USS Meteor (1863) was a gunboat the Federal Navy had acquired during the war. She carried heavy artillery and became part of the sea blockade of the waterways of the former Confederate states.

As they traveled down the river, the gloomy, bad-tempered feeling grew stronger as half the regiment rode on a small, light-draft river steamer heading for Hampton Roads via the James River. Just as the Corps had begun its journey down the river, the men on the lower deck began firing at objects on the shore. Colonel Garrard, who was on the upper deck, drew his revolver and started down to stop the firing. Taking Parson's advice, he explained the gunboat's purpose to the men, and some of them took heed. The argument was convincing, and he returned to the upper deck.

As recorded in Colonel Garrard's notes of what occurred, the men became disobedient, refusing to obey all orders, and continued firing at objects on the shore. Shortly after, they either ran out of ammunition or were tired of the sport, as they ceased firing. When Parson arrived at Hampton Roads, he boarded the USS Meteor, which was to take them to Texas. He learned that the other half of the regiment had also mutinied on their way down the river. The Federal Army abstained from giving publicity to exceptional cases, not wishing to fuel the prejudice that existed against the employment of Black men as soldiers.

The mutiny ended when the whole regiment got together on the decks of the Meteor. On June 16, 1865, 16,000 USCT veterans of the XXV Corps arrived at Brazos Santiago from City Point, Virginia, arriving at anchor at noon on June 30, 1865. Authorities quickly dispersed them to Fort Brown in Brownsville, Ringgold Barracks in Rio Grande City, Fort McIntosh in Laredo, and Fort Duncan in Eagle Pass. They established smaller posts at their assigned locations to prevent former Confederates from reforming their defeated government and Army in Mexico.

During encampment in Brazos Santiago, Texas, Parson could not help but think about any open hostilities in Southampton County and the humanitarian relief challenges. Parson found that the military Reconstruction duty in Virginia presented rewards and challenges. He wondered how he and his parents, Solomon, and Louisa, would manage their newly gained freedom on Jacob's farm in Southampton County.

On January 5, 1866, Congress passed the Freedmen's Bureau Act of 1866, thereby further establishing the Bureau. In addition, it encompassed formerly enslaved people and refugees everywhere in the United States, not just in former Confederate states. The bill also expanded the power of military governors to enforce provisions aimed at protecting Black Americans. It defined the organization of interim governments in the South under conditions prescribed by Congress.

While the Bureau for the Relief of Freedmen and Refugees Act of 1865 was a considerable legislative accomplishment, it limited the agency's operation to just one year after the Civil War. The Freedmen Bureau's work consisted chiefly of five kinds of activity. It comprised relief work for both Black people and whites in the war-stricken former Confederate areas. Additionally, it included regulating Black labor under new conditions, administering justice in cases involving Black people, managing abandoned and confiscated property, and supporting education for Black settlements.

The Second Freedmen's Bureau Act was a Republican effort to extend the life and expand the duties of the Freedmen's Bureau that was established by law in March 1865. Republicans hoped to provide people of color with the economic and educational opportunities they believed necessary for equal citizenship. The Freedmen's Bureau Act of 1866 became law on July 16, extending the work of the agency for two more years.

Subsequently, state and local governments developed laws to regulate the activities of newly freed Black people. Some laws protected them, particularly those relating to labor contracts, but others circumscribed their citizenship rights. While a significant part of the Bureau's early activities involved supervising abandoned and confiscated property, its primary mission was to provide relief and help formerly enslaved people become self-sufficient. As Congress extended the life of the Bureau, it added other duties, such as assisting Black soldiers and sailors in obtaining back pay, bounty payments, and pensions.

Knowing about the Freedmen's Bureau Act of 1866 in the Department of Virginia, the state superintendent, and district agents eased Parson's mind. Nevertheless, he had some worries about how the Freedmen's Bureau Act of 1866 was implemented and its activities in Southampton County. After Parson met Chaplain Turner, he learned about the local agents who assisted freed individuals in negotiating and upholding labor agreements in the post-war for-hire labor market.

In Texas, he grieved for Solomon and Louisa. He wanted to know who would protect them and whether they would be effective in doing so. Parson made sure that the local agents traveled to the Black settlement where Solomon and Louisa lived in Southampton County. Occasionally, the agents intervened in legal disputes to safeguard their freedoms. Establishing schools and hiring teachers for freedpeople in the county was Parson's primary focus.

In the state, Parson carried out civil-military and humanitarian duties, offering support and supplies to formerly enslaved Black people. Parson gathered enough information and support for the soldiers of the 1st Cavalry Regiment, USCT, with families living in Southampton County, prompting warranted intervention from Bureau officials. The agents revealed to him that both Black people and whites in the county were outspoken about issues of race, civil rights, and full equality for the newly freed population.

Specifically, Parson's concerns centered on whether General Brown, Assistant Commissioner in Virginia, and district agents working within the county took measures to address violence against Black people. In Texas, he observed how the absence of practical freedom compelled emancipated Black people to seek protection and enforcement of laws. Parson acquired communication and people skills that enabled him to advocate for the essential life lessons, as well as the behavioral skills needed to face full emancipation. Eventually, he learned that the Bureau agents in Southampton County issued thousands of emergency rations immediately after the suspension of open hostilities.

Parson drew inspiration from his mentors, who served as a vital link between the high-level politics of Reconstruction and his day-to-day experiences. During his journey of self-liberation, he became a champion for true-life freedom. Parson gained confidence, insight, advice, training, and interpersonal skills to overcome his initial fears and face the transition toward promoting freedom, citizenship, and equality. No longer alarmed by the chaos and tensions in post-Civil War Virginia, Parson overcame self-doubt and regained his confidence.

During the pause in open war hostilities, Parson started a broader discussion about inclusive citizenship and voting rights for everyone. Considering how civil-military operations affected his life, he had his reasons for his views, including personal, social, economic, and political experiences. These included military actions against irregular forces that violently opposed the Federal Army's rule. Their efforts to restore white supremacy and enslave Black people again deeply disturbed Parson.

Parson relentlessly advocated and pursued education, politics, and complete citizenship from enslavement to freedom. With the passage of the Freedmen's Bureau Acts of 1865 and 1866 by Congress, Parson felt less pressure. Congress ensured that the acts achieved more than aiding the freed people. The agency's first action was to help war victims and refugees of all backgrounds, both Black and white, with a close eye on the civil-military operations.

In Virginia, white people reacted with hostility and resentment to the Federal troops and the Bureau. They viewed it as an overreach of federal power and an attempt to interfere with their social and economic order. Many saw the Bureau's efforts to assist newly freed Black people as a direct challenge to their way of life and a threat to their control over the labor force. Complaints from white citizens in Virginia led to the removal of most Black troops from the state.

Parson's unwavering commitment to his self-liberation made confronting the racist opposition unavoidable, and there was no turning back. He felt prepared to cross the color line that separated life in Southampton County from the anticipated promises of emancipation. Restoring agriculture was the most pressing task, with long-term implications. The deployment to Texas revealed many of the restrictive laws designed to limit the freedom of Black Americans, and many of the issues surrounding Reconstruction that persist in society today.

CHAPTER THREE

The Thirteenth Amendment Ratified

The war forever changed Parson's world—a war that was supposed to break the country apart, but in the end, stitched his own story together. He was stubborn, yes, but it was more than that. The violence he had seen, the questions he had dared to ask, and the weight of the battles he had survived had all carved something new into him. That has kept him in uniform for three long years, even when hope felt thin.

On January 31, Congress had passed the Thirteenth Amendment. Months before Booth would steal Lincoln from the country, lawmakers in Washington demanded that the Southern states, battered and angry, sign on if they wanted a seat at the table again. Word first reached Parson and the others in the freezing winter of 1865, the way news always did: through rumor, through a preacher's trembling voice, through the hush that fell over a church when the news was just too big to hold inside.

The Emancipation Proclamation had made grand promises, but everyone in church knew it was a wartime decree, slippery as a river stone. No, the country needed something heavier, something that could not be swept away by the next President or the next wave of violence. The Amendment—real, legal, carved into the bones of the Constitution—was the only way to end enslavement for good. It was a fight, every inch. Congress had to battle for votes, wrestle with the old order, and promise to enforce the new law by any means necessary.

On December 6, 1865, the church bell rang out the news: the Amendment had been ratified by twenty-seven states, enough to become law. President Lincoln was gone, but his successor, Andrew Johnson, had pushed the last Southern states—Alabama, North Carolina, Georgia—to accept the new reality. Enslavement was banned everywhere the U.S. flag flew, except, it turned out, for those convicted of a crime. The words were plain: "neither enslavement nor involuntary servitude, except as a punishment for a crime whereof the party shall have been duly convicted, shall exist within the United States, or any place subject to its jurisdiction."

It was a day for celebration, but it was not simple. Solomon and Louisa, sitting in the back pew, understood what most did not: the words that freed them also left a crack in the door. That exception—punishment for a crime—would let future generations twist the law, turning prison sentences into chains that looked an awful lot like the old ones. It was a bitter truth, hiding inside a victory, and it is one that Americans still argue about in every generation.

After the Amendment, the game changed, but the rules did not. Southern authorities started arresting Black men and women for "crimes" so vague they might as well have been invented on the spot—malicious mischief, loitering, anything that kept them in line. Then came convict leasing. The same fields, the same work, only now the master paid the state instead of the enslaved. Solomon and Louisa called it "enslavement by another name." Even now, the debate rages on.

In their settlement, everything important revolved around the church. If you wanted to see Solomon and Louisa, you went there. They spent hours inside those rough wooden walls, singing, praying, planning. The church was more than a building. It was a gathering place, a school, a meeting hall, and sometimes even a courtroom. The pastors were teachers, politicians, and business leaders — the heart and mind of the community — even if they only made it out once or twice a month. The Amendment and the church together gave people a way to imagine a future, to fight for rights Congress had finally promised, even if the country was still learning how to keep those promises.

Enslavement was not a ghost that disappeared overnight. Its shadow stretched across every field and street. Congress had left the exception in the law as a compromise—practical, they said. But compromise always comes with consequences. During Reconstruction, lawmakers argued and protested, trying to decide if they had done the right thing or just changed the chains.

Down in Southampton County, Solomon and Louisa saw how the loophole worked. The new "laws" targeted Black Americans, sending them to jail for nothing at all, then sending them right back to the fields. The so-called freedom came with conditions, and everyone knew who was meant to suffer.

For Parson, the end of enslavement was never just a headline or a law. It hit him deep, reshaping what he believed about freedom. Lincoln's words at Gettysburg echoed in his mind, but now Parson understood them in his bones. He spent long nights talking with Chaplain Henry McNeal Turner, learning what Reconstruction might offer—the hope and the danger. The surrounding violence never really went away. Sometimes it was a knife in the dark, sometimes a whisper, sometimes just the fear that clung to daylight. But Parson felt, more and more, that his own voice mattered, that he could help build the world Lincoln had promised.

He learned about the Amendment's journey: the House passed it on January 31, Lincoln signed it, and sent it to the states. By March's end, nineteen states had ratified it. By the day Lincoln died—April 14—only twenty-one had done so. The president's death was not just a tragedy; it was a turning point, a reminder of how fragile freedom could be. Parson saw his mission anew: not just to survive, but to fight for something larger—citizenship, equality, a place at the table.

Sergeant Etheridge dreamed of a clean break from the past, a quick political cure. Johnson, the new president, wanted something slower: a careful hand-off from military to civilian rule, letting the old order fade out bit by bit. Under Johnson, the

Army stayed on as a buffer, stepping in only if chaos threatened to spill over. But once civilian governments returned, Johnson wanted his soldiers gone, leaving the states to their own devices. The Army, he said, would only act if the peace broke, and even then, only as a last resort.

President Johnson maintained his stance until Congress convened in December 1865. On December 18, 1865, Congress ratified the constitutional Amendment, abolishing enslavement throughout the United States. This was the first of three Reconstruction amendments to the U.S. Constitution, giving Congress new authority to define and protect civil rights at the federal level.

For Parson, real freedom was more than the absence of chains. It was the chance to choose, to learn, to live without someone else's hand on your shoulder. He read newspapers, leafed through old pamphlets, watched the world change and wondered what would come next. Justice, citizenship, equality, these were the promises, but he knew they'd have to be fought for, every day. The Thirteenth Amendment was not just a line in a book. It was a door opening, and Parson was determined to step through.

The Emancipation Proclamation, issued by President Lincoln, has historically overshadowed the ratification of the constitutional Amendment. While Lincoln understood the wrongfulness of enslavement, he acted to avoid provoking those border states that had remained to support the Federal government. Lincoln's proclamation freed only those enslaved in Confederate states where he and the Federal Army could not force the issue. Still, it allowed enslavement to continue in states where the Federal government could impose its will. The proclamation galvanized Congressional abolitionists into redoubling their commitment to the complete abolition of enslavement across the former Confederacy.

Parson envisioned land ownership, imagining fields of cotton swaying in rich, freshly tilled soil. He dreamed of food production, with harvests in his hands, and the joyful sounds of plump chickens clucking. However, the war's impact on land and labor in the separated states was clear from the beginning. As enslavement was gradually eased during wartime, a long, and challenging process of rebuilding life and work began for both Black people and whites. In Black communities, landownership, and food production were the goals of formerly enslaved individuals. Their hopes, like those of rural folks everywhere, revolved around subsistence farming—growing enough food for their families and selling some extra crops. Working for themselves, rather than being enslaved by a white person, was especially meaningful to them.

Their visions were on display in the famous meeting between Major General William T. Sherman and a group of Black religious leaders in Savannah, Georgia. On January 12, 1865, Sherman and Secretary of War Edwin M. Stanton asked a group of Black ministers what the freed people wanted. Reverend Garrison Frazier responded that freedom meant. He said, "taking us from under the yoke of bondage and placing us where we can reap the fruit of our labor, take care of ourselves, and assist the Government in maintaining our freedom."

On January 16, 1865, General Sherman issued his wartime Special Field Orders, No. 15. He ordered the Army to allot land to some freed families, in plots of land no larger than 40 acres, and to lend mules for the agrarian reform effort. The field orders provided for the confiscation of 400,000 acres of land along the Atlantic coast of South Carolina, Georgia, and Florida, and the dividing of it into parcels of not more than forty acres. The government promised to settle approximately 18,000 formerly enslaved families and other Black people then living in the area.

Just four days after meeting with the Black leaders, Lincoln approved Field Order No. 15, which Sherman had not yet issued. This crucial 1865 meeting sparked a bold and sweeping plan to change land and labor in the Confederate states. Once Field Order No. 15 was approved, freedpeople immediately started settling on land and farming for themselves. By the end of the war, they had established farms and communities on land in places like Roanoke Island, North Carolina, and near Norfolk, Virginia.

During the Reconstruction era in the seceded states, military posts, and stations meticulously documented and reported on martial law operations and organizations. Black settlements, both large and small, rely on word of mouth and newspapers to learn about agents' daily activities and their own social, political, and economic situations. The pastors were often the settlement leaders, teachers, news reporters, and business strategists. Families usually spent many hours at the church each week or when the preacher came to their settlement, sometimes only once or twice a month, to learn and hear about the daily activities.

Under the Reconstruction Act of 1867, the Freedmen's Bureau's Washington headquarters established subordinate headquarters stations and field offices in each of the five designated Military Districts, each under the command of a major general. After Major General Howard was appointed the Commissioner of the Bureau, he designated Assistant Commissioners for each of the states. Consequently, they appointed officers to oversee the Bureau's work in each county and city.

The Bureau headquarters files document the overall administration and operation of the Bureau, its education division, and the supervision of field offices. Records include letters, telegrams, and circular letters sent; special orders issued by Commissioner Oliver O. Howard; annual reports to the President; records relating to appointments; and letters received by the Commissioner. They comprised reports from the State Assistant Commissioners on relief efforts. They included hospitals and vaccination programs, labor, and land issues, legal matters, field office management, school reports, school schedules, and rental accounts from state superintendents of education.

The records of State Assistant Commissioners include copies of letters and annual reports sent to the Commissioner in Washington, D.C. They also contain narrative summaries of problems and developments in the state. The records feature letters received from subordinates in field offices, telegrams, and issuances from Washington. They included narrative reports on topics such as the condition of the destitute, misuse of public stores, status of Bureau property, abandoned and confiscated lands, murders, and outrages, and other areas of concern. Additionally, there are forms on schools, labor, and personnel records, returns from medical officers, and correspondence.

Field office records, organized by state, contain field office reports, letters received and sent, contracts, certificates, registers, censuses, affidavits, and other documents. The field offices of the Bureau provided direct assistance to and contact with the formerly enslaved who were seeking relief. Besides letters and accounts directly from freed people, these records also contain documents from employers, landowners, and others who participated in the mission of helping the formerly enslaved become self-sufficient.

The records were rich in names and personal information of individuals whose correspondence included marriage certificates, educational records, labor contracts, hospital records, complaints, relief rolls, land applications, requests for legal aid and protection, and trial summaries.

In February 1866, the 1st Regiment, Cavalry, USCT, having finished its service on the Rio Grande and at various locations in Texas, returned to Virginia. Parson left the Rio Grande with the 1st Regiment, USCT Cavalry, and went back to Fort Monroe, Virginia, where he enlisted. The end of the war marked the rebuilding of the Federal government and the abolition of chattel enslavement by the nation. A provisional military government set up in the county pursued a peaceful, protective, and supportive policy.

The officers of the 1st Regiment USCT Cavalry, their voices crisp and clear against the soundscape of Fort Monroe, informed the soldiers of imminent army situations. They spoke of the day's tasks, explaining their place within the complex waves of social, political, and military affairs already anticipated. They detailed the potential engagements with irregular insurgents encamped in the area. The records on the local Black settlements were rich in names and personal information of individuals. The correspondence included marriage certificates, educational records, labor contracts, hospital records, complaints, relief rolls, land applications, requests for legal aid and protection, and trial summaries.

The first decade of Black emancipation in Virginia established a foundation. This foundation proved crucial for the advancement of Black literacy. Its architects were Virginia's formerly enslaved men and women who were determined that they and their children would possess the knowledge necessary for freedom and citizenship. Attempts by the state government to reassert policies of white supremacy complicated their efforts, and the Federal government did not appropriate adequate funds to public education. The government's withdrawal of support left the educational system unfinished.

Emancipation and the ratification of the constitutional Amendment radically altered labor, social, and political relations between the races. Black expectations of personal, political, and economic freedom after the war collided with white resistance. Many whites, embittered by the war and desperately clinging to an antebellum model of race relations, used violence to enforce labor contracts, social mores, and claims to political supremacy. Republican leaders in Congress initiated several provisions to help protect the rights of freed people.

Virginia's formerly enslaved citizens pursued education for themselves and their children as soon as they could. Soon after the war started in Virginia, Black people set up and taught in schools for Virginia's freed population. A Black American Virginian established the state's first Black secondary school. Over one-third of the teachers at Virginia's first Black schools between 1861 and the end of Reconstruction were Black. They served much longer in schools for formerly enslaved people in Virginia than white teachers, whether north or south.

Emancipated Black people put aside their enslavement and embraced education, hard work, faith, and citizenship with extraordinary enthusiasm and devotion. By 1868, over 80 percent of Black men who were eligible to vote had registered, schools for Black children had become a priority, and courageous Black leaders had overcome enormous obstacles to win elections to public office.

Not only were Black people the first to teach in primary schools for Virginia's freed people, but they also founded and staffed the state's first secondary school for free Black people. Northern aid societies, such as the American Missionary Association (AMA), sent teachers, books, and other educational support to Virginia's early Black schools. The Federal government also provided building materials for schools and transportation for northern teachers through the Freedmen's Bureau.

The agency established schools for formerly enslaved people, women, children, and poor whites. The most visible success of the Bureau and its associates was the establishment of Historically Black Colleges and Universities (HBCUs). The General Assembly, which comprised approximately thirty Black representatives, passed a comprehensive school law in late 1870, establishing the positions of Superintendent of Public Instruction and a state Board of Education. The law authorized these new offices to appoint local superintendents and hire teachers for the new schools. The new constitution also required the legislature to devote a portion of the state's tax revenue to support the new school system.

While in Texas, Parson first encountered the terrifying reality of widespread terrorism carried out by the KKK, who disguised themselves in white robes and operated covertly at night across the former Confederate states. Dressed in a false sense of brotherhood, these political and social terrorists secretly organized as a social group in Pulaski, Tennessee, in 1866. Some say the name Klu Klux Klan comes from the Greek "kyklos," meaning "circle," and is the origin of the English word. The frightening name resonated through the small town.

At the start of the occupation, the Army deployed about 20,000 troops throughout the South, who protected polling sites and performed other peacekeeping duties. In 1865 and 1866, the

U.S. Army maintained a steadily shrinking number of posts in the seceded states. At one point, about half of this occupation force comprised USCT who had joined the Federal Army late in the war. Their commanders often stationed them in remote areas to appease the anger or anxiety of Southern whites.

According to Union Army findings, the KKK's origins were in a social club formed by Confederate veterans. The organization rapidly transformed into a tool for clandestine white Southern resistance against Radical Reconstruction. Through intimidation and violence, Klan members aimed to reestablish white supremacy over newly enfranchised Black people. With the passage of the Reconstruction Acts in March 1867 and the prospect of formerly enslaved people voting in the South, the Klan became a political organization.

The Army identified Nathan Bedford Forrest as the first grand wizard, followed by grand dragons, grand titans, and grand cyclops in a hierarchical order. In the summer of 1867, delegates from former Confederate states met at a convention in Nashville, Tennessee, to establish the KKK as the "Invisible Empire of the South." Forrest, a former Confederate cavalry general, presided over the convention. They wore robes and sheets to conceal their identities from federal troops and to intimidate Black people. The KKK carried out nighttime attacks and murders against formerly enslaved people and their White allies.

The Klan designed most of its terrorist actions to intimidate Black voters and white Republican Party supporters. Klansmen paraded on horseback at night dressed in outlandish costumes, or they might threaten specific Republican leaders with violence. Increasingly during 1868, these actions became violent, ranging from whippings of Black women perceived as insolent to the assassination of Republican leaders.

Terrified whispers echoing through the streets served as a stark testament to the dreadful pogrom that had gripped the Black settlement. It was impossible to separate local vigilante violence from political terrorism organized by the Klan. Attacks on Black people became frequent in 1868. Freedmen's Bureau agents reported 336 cases of murder or assault intended to kill formerly enslaved people across the state from January 1 to November 15, 1868. This led Congress to pass bills authorizing the President to suspend the writ of habeas corpus, use force to suppress disturbances, and impose severe penalties on terrorist organizations.

In 1867, President Johnson appointed General Schofield as the military governor of Virginia. He supervised the elections in which both Black and white voters participated, leading to the Virginia Constitutional Convention of 1868. When Radicals took control of that convention and proposed disenfranchising former Confederates, Schofield raised concerns about corruption with Congress and his commander, General Ulysses Grant. Although the Army enforced congressional mandates that allowed Black people to participate in the political process fully, most state offices in Virginia remained held by white native Virginians.

By March 1867, Radical Republicans in Congress had become deeply frustrated with President Johnson's policies, which, they believed, allowed too many former Confederates to hold public office in the South. Politically empowered former Confederates would obstruct the civil rights of newly freed Black people, and for Republicans, those rights, which would allow abolition to translate to absolute freedom, were critical. As a result, the radical Republican majority in Congress passed several essential bills over the President's veto.

In 1868, President Johnson assigned Major General Stoneman to administer the military government in the sub-district of Petersburg, Virginia, and he assumed command of the Military District One. Stoneman, a Democrat who opposed the radical Reconstruction, pursued more moderate policies than the other military governors, which garnered him support among white Virginians. Freedpeople found more of an ally in Major General George Stoneman than in his predecessor.

In 1869, General Canby became the military governor of Virginia. Shortly after arriving in Richmond, he took control of all the city's medical facilities and repurposed them for the Union Army. Over the following months, Canby recognized the urgent medical and economic crisis faced by thousands of formerly enslaved Black people in the state who the Civil War had uprooted. He faced the challenge of providing Black people with access to health and mental health services while trying to maintain the racial hierarchy that existed in the South.

To Parson, the Army was a north star of steely blue and brassy inspiration, guiding decision-making and enforcing congressional mandates. These mandates, like promising cherry blooms, failed to always grant Black people full political participation. Yet, in the fragrant fields and stately assembly halls of Virginia, white natives, their voices echoing with generations of power, still grasped the reins of most state offices. The air hung heavily with racial tension, a perceived political force against the promise of change.

On April 7, 1866, the President directed Generals John Steedman and Joseph Fullerton to investigate the operations of the Freedmen's Bureau in the seceded states. They performed inspections of the duties conducted in the departments of Virginia and North Carolina. They submitted the following report of their observations. In Virginia, they assessed and reported the numbers of military officers and other people working for or connected to the Bureau.

The Commissioners reported one colonel, two lieutenant colonels, three majors, one captain and commissary of subsistence, nine captains and assistant quartermasters, nineteen captains of the line, twenty-three first lieutenants, and twenty-second lieutenants working for the Bureau. They found 233 civilian employees. This included fifty-eight classified clerks and superintendents of farms, twelve as assistant superintendents, and 163 classified as laborers. In addition, the Bureau employed enlistees in the military service as orderlies and guards. Still, it did not procure the number of those soldiers.

In the former Confederate states, there were settlements made up entirely of colonies of formerly enslaved people, numbering thousands, and living in truly deplorable conditions. These unfortunate individuals entered our lines and stayed there throughout the war. They lived in small, hand-built huts made from lumber. Each of these huts was just a single room, often shared by large families. The assistant superintendent of the Bureau for the settlement supervised the colony.

The Commissioners visited all the important cities and towns, as well as the headquarters of each district of the Bureau in Virginia. They also took advantage of every opportunity to talk with and gather the opinions of citizens they met on the streets, in taverns, and while traveling on trains.

Between May 1866 and January 1868, Second Lieutenant A. G. Deacon, a native of Fond du Lac, Wisconsin, served as a Freedmen's Bureau agent in Southampton. In 1867, he also held a key role as President of the Board of Registration, which was responsible for enrolling Black voters while excluding whites who could not meet specific wartime loyalty tests. Deacon's time in Southampton coincided with a shift in federal Reconstruction policy from a passive to a more active approach. His second position in the summer of 1867 symbolized an expanded federal effort to bring about change in the South. By examining Lieutenant Deacon's activities, Parson gained valuable insight into his role both as a Bureau agent and as a federal registrar.

As a Bureau agent, Lieutenant Deacon had three principal responsibilities. First, he promoted free-labor agriculture, especially by arranging contracts between formerly enslaved people and landowners. Second, he encouraged the development of schools. Finally, he served as a judicial officer, attending preliminary hearings and trials in local court cases involving Black people as parties. He exercised discretionary jurisdiction over lesser cases and recommended the transfer of significant cases to military courts.

The last of these three functions might have been the Bureau agent's most significant public responsibility: that of an ombudsman overseeing the local judicial system. These judicial duties involved him in various cases that collectively highlight the issues where disputes most often arose during the early postwar years. Freedmen sued landowners for unpaid wages, property such as animals and clothing, and control over Black children, many of whom were bound out through apprenticeships. Lieutenant Deacon also had to handle incidents of violence and forcible evictions of formerly enslaved people.

Many obstacles hindered the development of free-labor agriculture. During the first few years after the war, formerly enslaved people often complained about being cheated out of wages. They could sue successfully in the court of formerly enslaved people. According to the Bureau's records, in 1866, Lyman Parker and Richard White recovered $5 and $15, respectively. Frank Lee received only $14 for a full seven months of work. Disputes over possessions frequently arose. The court for formerly enslaved people in Southampton ruled against several landowners who allegedly withheld promised clothing and wages. Other formerly enslaved people took legal action to recover animals. Mary Jones and Boling H. Ricks each recovered a cow, and Fannie Ricks regained custody of a pig.

The formerly enslaved people had less success in recovering apprenticed children. A Black woman who had been free before the war hopes, under the new order of things, to reclaim a son, who remained indentured to a white person until the age of twenty-one. Lieutenant Deacon sent an inquiry about the case to his superiors. They said, "The woman had better stand by her contracts. It is not the policy of this Bureau to disallow contracts unless very unfavorable." Nancy Artis recovered from Stephen Henderson.

Still, the prominent Thomas Ridley defended himself against a legal challenge from Peter Johnson, a formerly enslaved person Ridley held, whose daughter was the child's former owner. The formerly enslaved people's court ruled that Ridley had provided "good and kind treatment" to Johnson's daughter and his other formerly enslaved individuals. Therefore, he should keep her in his service until she turned eighteen. In return, Ridley agreed to pay her $15 per year to teach her to read and write and to supply her with proper food, clothing, shelter, and medical care.

These cases opened the door to widespread abuse. Over the next several years, the county court arbitrarily apprenticed large numbers of Black children without regard for their parents' wishes. It seems unlikely that the beneficiaries kept their promises to teach the children to read and write.

Three years after his emancipation, Parson returned to Southampton County, prepared to cross the racial gateway onto Jacob's farm. It was a time of complex adjustments and some noteworthy accomplishments. Virginians of all backgrounds attempted to rebuild in the radically new conditions that the defeat of the Confederacy and the abolition of enslavement produced. The military occupation of the county faced poverty and poor relief challenges under Sub-assistant Commissioner Lieutenant A. G. Deacon (4th Division, 1st Subdistrict). The military appointed governors and controlled the state while the General Assembly was not in session.

Emancipation radically altered labor, social, and political relations between the races. Black expectations of personal, political, and economic freedom after the war ran recklessly into white resistance. Many whites, embittered by the war and desperately clinging to an antebellum model of race relations, used violence to enforce labor contracts, social mores, and claims to political supremacy. Republican leaders in Congress initiated a few provisions to help protect the rights of formerly enslaved people.

Parson felt ready to cross the gateway that separated the races. Living in the low-lying plains of southeastern Virginia and away from the coast, Black and white folks' businesses centered around farming. As the top cotton-growing county, the smell of cotton and rich earth filled Southampton's vast fields. Peanuts increased their agricultural importance, leading to a much larger hog population than other livestock. Corn and hay were also vital crops. Like in all the strict agrarian counties of the state, the towns were small and spread out, and their populations were far less than those of the rural areas.

The personal, labor, social, and environmental conditions of southeastern Virginia were key economic factors in farming. Parson learned from Solomon that fruiting trees needed cool temperatures to grow and break dormancy. Unlike sweet cherries, sour cherries were more resilient and could better withstand winter weather. According to him, Solomon advised picking cherries from trees located in frost-protected areas near houses or on slightly higher ground. Similarly, he learned that the newly freed workers required fair labor treatment to truly achieve freedom.

The blooming of cherry trees brought a sense of renewal, and it reminded Parson that each victory by federal troops reaffirmed the promise of freedom. Inspired by this, Parson felt dedicated both to navigating the complex path toward complete emancipation in the seceded states and to his own self-liberation, a journey from which there was no turning back. Just as the barren cherry trees required proper agricultural practices,

In Southampton County, issues in the farming business arise from personal, labor, social, and political relations between the races. The Army had to make sure that landowners paid these returning workers fairly and treated them as the formerly enslaved people they now were. To encourage formerly enslaved people to go back to the farms they had previously worked. To strengthen the system further, the Army distributed abandoned, captured, and surplus government horses and mules to the community.

The constitutional end of enslavement, legally abolished enslavement in all states, and the status of over half a million Black people in Virginia began to change. They looked forward to the changes promised, including the fruits of education, political participation, and full citizenship, after being enslaved.

Yet, in their struggle to achieve these goals, Black men and women faced the hostilities of their former masters and the society that had long benefited from their unpaid labor.

In 1865, when the war ended, Congress still had not settled the issue of enslavement for the entire country. During the debates over Reconstruction, the nation ratified the Thirteenth Amendment and established the Freedmen's Bureau. The constitutional Amendment addressed a problem that had remained unresolved since the country's founding. Its legacy has allowed for more extensive efforts to review and amend previous actions.

The Federal government required the former Confederate states to include the abolition of enslavement in their new state constitutions. Still, besides banning enslavement, the Amendment outlawed the practice of involuntary servitude and peonage. Nothing prevented states from re-instituting the practice with revised state constitutions. Through the Black Codes, Virginia subjugated both enslaved and free Black Americans, thereby resulting in their sustained oppression in Southampton County.

As Parson learned, the Amendment did not end discrimination or protect Black people from violence. His victory in the Civil War, however, renewed and secured Parson's future. Over half a million Black people in Virginia asked, now that we have freedom at the national level, what are we going to do with it?

CHAPTER FOUR

The First Reconstruction Act

February 1866 dawned quietly, so unlike the way Parson had grown used to measuring time—by the sharp bursts of cannon, by the ragged shouts of men, by the sudden, lurching gallop of his own pulse in the thick of battle. He left the Rio Grande with his regiment, the 1st USCT Cavalry, boots already worn thin, scars running deeper than he cared to admit. He returned to Fort Monroe as if waking from a fever dream, trudging through the familiar gates that had marked the start of his journey just over a year before.

The war was over, or so everyone kept saying. The air at Fort Monroe, once sharp with the tang of gunpowder and the iron-sweet smell of blood, was oddly still now. The fields outside the fort were littered with the ghosts of old battles, spent shells, shattered fences, churned-up earth. The silence was its own kind of weight, pressing against Parson's ribs. It was hard to believe that all those years of chaos had led to this—the quiet aftermath, the uncertain future.

Still, for Parson and the men he called brothers, the Army was more than a uniform. It was the only institution standing between them and the raw, unpredictable anger of a defeated South. The old world had been ripped up by its roots—towns burned, families scattered, the system of enslavement that had defined their lives now in ruins. Freedom had come suddenly, but what it meant, what it would look like, what it would cost—was still a question with no clear answer.

He remembered the day the news reached them: August 20, 1866. President Johnson had issued his proclamation, standing before the nation to declare that the insurrection was ended and that peace, order, and tranquility had returned. The words sounded hollow to Parson. He had seen too much, felt too much. Texas was still holding out, but everywhere else, the Union insisted, the war was finished. It was time to stitch the country back together, to act like it had never been torn apart.

Parson did not feel peace. He felt a kind of numbness, a waiting. He watched as the old Confederacy buckled under the weight of its own defeat. The physical destruction was everywhere, and the social world that had kept Parson and millions of others in bondage had collapsed. But nothing new had yet been built to take its place. The government, the Army, the very men who'd once called themselves masters—all of them seemed confused, scrambling to find some new order that made sense.

In February 1867, Congress took its own stand. The First Reconstruction Act was passed, spelling out what the Southern states would have to do if they wanted to rejoin the Union.

Parson read about it in the newspapers, in the official circulars pinned up in the barracks. President Johnson fought it tooth and nail, insisting that mercy was the better path. He wanted to wipe away old debts, pardon the Confederates, welcome them back with a handshake if they'd just say a few right words. But Congress demanded more: new constitutions, abolition in writing, a genuine commitment to change.

At Fort Monroe, politics was not just something that happened in Washington. It was personal. It was about who could vote, who could speak, who could shape the future. Black men—men like Parson, men who had bled for the Union—wanted their say. At the same time, many white Virginians, loyal to the Confederacy, found themselves banned from the ballot box. Some got their rights back thanks to the General Assembly, but only if they bent the knee, swore allegiance, or begged for a pardon from the President. The ground beneath everyone's feet seemed to shift daily, the rules changing with every new proclamation.

Freedom, for the first time, felt almost within reach. The old order was gone; the new one was still being written. Black men in Virginia, for the first time, could imagine themselves as citizens, not just survivors. Parson believed in that vision with every fiber of his being. To him, freedom was nothing less than the full rights of citizenship: to own land, to vote, to hold office, to be seen and heard and counted as a man.

But the war's bitterness lingered. White Southerners, stripped of their power and pride, did not surrender their hatred. Parson saw the rise of new monsters—hooded men, secret societies like the Klan and the Knights of the White Camellia, who attacked in the night, burned homes, lynched men, terrorized Black communities, and white Republicans alike. They meant to drag the South backwards, to keep men like Parson in fear, to erase any progress that had been made.

The year after the war, there was no peace; it was a storm. The Reconstruction Act forced changes, but the violence only grew into riots, lynchings, and open massacres, all across the ravaged South. Radical Republican governments tried desperately to hold things together, to solve the problems left behind by the war and the collapse of slavery. But it was like trying to patch a sinking ship in the middle of a storm.

Parson's own journey back to Fort Monroe in December 1865 was a strange homecoming. The old fort looked the same—thick stone walls, sentries pacing at dawn—but everything else had changed. Congress and the President fought openly, passing laws and vetoes, imposing military rule on the South. Parson read every scrap of news he could find, hungry for some sign of hope. The Fourteenth Amendment was the new litmus test: no state would be readmitted until it guaranteed civil rights for all.

His time as a soldier had not left Parson wounded, but it had changed him. He felt he had earned something bigger than a discharge. He had earned the right to all the promises of citizenship—freedom, property, the vote, the right to stand as an equal among men. He was glad to be done with the endless patrols along the Texas border, but Virginia was no sanctuary. Racism was a beast with a thousand mouths, and everyone seemed to spit venom. The violence in Norfolk and Richmond was relentless, the air thick with rumors and fear. Parson worried that the same men who had fought to keep him a slave would soon run the state again, thanks to President Johnson's easy forgiveness. But he refused to be beaten down. He kept pressing forward, determined not just to survive, but to claim what was rightfully his.

He had not always been so sure of himself. At first, he had carried the weight of inferiority, a sense that he had to prove himself over and over. But the struggle—on the field, in the streets, in his own heart—had shaped him. He learned to speak up, to fight not just with fists or rifles, but with words. His confidence grew, and as it did, he inspired others. His journey became something larger—an example, a spark, a reminder that the fight for freedom was not over.

Fort Monroe itself was both a sanctuary and a reminder. The land all around bore the scars of war—shattered homes, burned fields, the bones of old plantations. The old society, built on the backs of men like Parson, was gone, but nothing had replaced it. The question hung over everything: how would the South be rebuilt? Who would decide what came next, and what role would the newly freed people play?

Every day, Parson faced the monstrous power of racial prejudice. He looked for allies wherever he could find them. Chaplain Henry McNeal Turner was one—a voice of wisdom, a man unafraid to speak truth in a place that often punished it. Parson learned to trust carefully, to measure a man by his actions, not his words. Company I, 1st Cavalry Regiment USCT, was a brotherhood, but outside the fort, danger lurked everywhere. Confederate sympathizers plotted in secret, and Parson knew he would have to fight again—not with bullets, but with determination, with hope, with the stubborn refusal to give up on the promise of freedom.

He found hope in others, too. In Norfolk, Black men gathered to form the Colored Monitor Union Club, demanding their rights. On May 25, 1865, over a thousand Black men marched to the polls, insisting on their right to vote. They published a pamphlet—Equal Suffrage: Address from the Colored Citizens of Norfolk, Va., to the People of the United States—declaring, "We simply ask that a Christian and enlightened people shall, at once, concede to us the full enjoyment of those privileges of full citizenship." Parson read every word, feeling the fire in their voices. They were not asking for charity or pity—they were demanding what was rightfully theirs.

The movement spread. In Hampton, Richmond, Williamsburg—across the state—Black men formed political clubs, held meetings, planned for a future they could never imagine. In August 1865, they convened a state convention in Alexandria, declaring that the laws of the Commonwealth should protect all men equally, demanding the right to vote as their inalienable right, promised by the Declaration of Independence.

White Virginians, meanwhile, clawed back their own rights, one by one. Union officials set rules for registering voters, trying to draw clear lines about who could participate. No Black men voted in the elections of 1865. The men chosen that year would serve until 1867, and Virginia would not send representatives to Congress until after Congressional Reconstruction ended in 1870.

Many in the Colored Monitor Union Club distrusted the Freedmen's Bureau, seeing it as just another layer of control, another set of restrictions. They wanted no more overseers, no more military "protection." They wanted freedom—not just from slavery, but from the constant interference of others.

One morning, Parson stood watch at the fort and saw a sight he never expected: the former Confederate President, Jefferson Davis, brought in as a prisoner. The government was taking no chances—Davis was chained, guarded day and night. Parson watched him with a strange feeling—part satisfaction, part sorrow. The man who had fought to keep Parson and his people enslaved now lived behind thick stone walls, while thousands of newly freed men built new lives in the shadow of the old rebellion.

Fort Monroe had once been called "Freedom Fortress," a beacon for families escaping slavery during the war. Now, just four years later, the man who had led the rebellion was here, locked away while more than 10,000 Black Americans lived in the area around the fort. The news of Davis's capture and imprisonment spread quickly—he was chained in a casemate for three days, guarded by federal soldiers, accused of treason, conspiracy, and cruelty to prisoners of war. The fort's walls, ten feet thick, had seen it all: the rise and fall of armies, the hope and heartbreak of a nation.

Davis spent six months in the casemate, then was moved to a cell inside Carroll Hall. After two years, he was released on bail, never tried. The government feared what might happen if a court had to decide whether the secession of 1860 and 1861 was legal. His capture, though, was a turning point—the final nail in the coffin of the Confederate dream.

For Parson, all of this—the politics, the violence, the hope, the fear—was not just history. It was life, lived day by day, breath by breath. His journey was not just about the battles he had fought with a rifle, but about the battles he fought within himself, and alongside his people, for the right to live free.

The struggle for human and civil rights was just beginning. Parson and those like him were not content with survival. They wanted dignity, respect, a future for their children. The Civil War had ended on the battlefield, but the real fight, the fight for equality, for justice, for the full promise of citizenship, was only beginning. And Parson, hardened by war but unbroken in spirit, was ready to meet it head-on.

During the 12 years of Reconstruction in Virginia, at least 2,000 Black women, men, and children fell victim to racial terrorism and lynchings. White perpetrators assaulted, raped, or injured thousands more in racial terror attacks between 1865 and 1876. Freedmen's Bureau field offices documented incidents of Reconstruction-era racial violence in forty Virginia counties.

Between 1865 and 1876, white mobs and individual Confederate sympathizers killed, attacked, assaulted, and terrorized thousands of Black women, men, and children, escaping arrest and prosecution. Society rarely held white perpetrators of lawless, random violence against formerly enslaved people accountable—instead, they often celebrated them.

Emboldened Confederate veterans and former enslavers organized a reign of terror that effectively nullified constitutional amendments designed to provide Black people equal protection and the right to vote. In a series of devastating decisions, the United States Supreme Court blocked Congressional efforts to protect formerly enslaved people. In decision after decision in the South, the Court ceded control to the same white people who used terror and violence to stop Black political participation. They upheld laws and practices that codified racial hierarchy and embraced a new constitutional order defined by states' rights.

Within a decade after the Civil War, Congress began to abandon the promise of assistance to millions of formerly enslaved Black people. Violence, mass lynchings, and lawlessness enabled white Southerners to create a regime of white supremacy and Black disenfranchisement alongside a new economic order that continued to exploit Black labor. White officials in the North and West rejected racial equality, codified racial discrimination, and occasionally embraced the same tactics of violent racial control seen in the former Confederacy.

Sympathetic white mobs and individuals across the former Confederate states engaged in widespread violence against Black settlements. These groups and individuals killed, attacked, assaulted, and terrorized thousands of Black women,

men, and children, often with impunity, escaping arrest and prosecution because of biased law enforcement and judicial systems. This wave of violence was fueled by racial animosity, a desire to maintain white supremacy, and resentment towards the newly gained rights and freedoms of formerly enslaved people.

Violence against formerly enslaved people was a widespread and tragic reality during the Congressional Reconstruction. White men and groups, often motivated by white supremacy and a desire to maintain the racial hierarchy that existed under enslavement, frequently attacked formerly enslaved people who were exercising their newfound freedom and civil rights. Parson recalled a Freedmen's Bureau report about a white man assaulted by a formerly enslaved person, whom he deemed impudent. The agency reported the following attack on a formerly enslaved person by a white man, who considered the formerly enslaved person impudent.

Major James Johnson
Assistant Commissioner
Brentsville, Virginia

January 15, 1866

Sir:

I have the honor to inform you that a dastardly outrage was committed in this place yesterday, (Sunday), within sight of my office, the circumstances of which are as follows.

A formerly enslaved person named James Cook was perceived as "impudent" by a white man named

John Cornwell, who cursed and threatened him. The formerly enslaved person, being alarmed, started away, and was followed and threatened with, "you Black Yankee, I will kill you." He was fired upon with a pistol, the ball passing through his clothes. He was then caught by the white man, beaten with the butt of a revolver, and dragged to the door of the Jail near where the affair occurred, where he was loosened and escaped.

He came to me soon after, bleeding from a deep cut over the eye, and reported the above, which was substantiated to me as fact by several witnesses. I have heard both sides of the case, and the only charge that is brought against the formerly enslaved person is "impudence," and while being pounced upon as a Yankee. While he cursed and called many names, this "impudence" consisted in the sole offense of saying that he had been in the Federal Army and was proud of it.

I know the formerly enslaved person well and know him to be intelligent, inoffensive, and respectful. He is an old gray-headed man and has been enslaved by the commonwealth attorney of this county for a long time. He has the reputation I have given him among the citizens here and has rented a farm near here for the coming season. As evidence of his peaceful disposition, he had a revolver, which was sold to him by the Government on his discharge from the Army. He did not draw or threaten to use during the assault, choosing, in this instance at least, to suffer wrong rather than to do wrong.

To show you the state of feeling here among many people, about such a transaction, Dr. C. H. Lambert, the practicing physician of this place, followed the formerly enslaved person to me. He says, "Subdued and miserable as we are, we will not allow Black people to come among us and brag about having been in the Yankee Army. It is as much as we can do to tolerate it in white men." He thought, "It would be a lesson to the Negroes."

Lieut. Marcus. S. Hopkins
Freedmen's Bureau Agent.

The above is a replicated report from the original Freedmen's Bureau records of a formerly enslaved person, attacked for impudence by a white man. Agents heard and reported many similar, and some more violent, remarks on this and other subjects connected with the formerly enslaved people. Hopkins would not convey the impression, however, that there was the slightest danger to any white man from the Black people. He said, "Whites held intense malice against the formerly enslaved person, from which he must be protected, or he will be worse off than when he was enslaved."

The April 1866 riot in Norfolk, Virginia, was the first significant postwar civil disturbance. On April 9, 1866, a crowd of Black people rallied to celebrate Congress' override of President Johnson's veto and the passage of the Civil Rights Act. They planned a larger rally and parade on April 16, 1866, combining Black people from both Portsmouth and Norfolk on the grounds near the latter city.

On April 12, 1866, Capt. Philip W. Stanhope, a battalion commander of the 12th United States Infantry commanding the posts of Norfolk and Portsmouth, learned that certain whites in Norfolk were planning to disrupt the celebration. They were former Confederates and members of a large, disorganized population of individuals who had been left behind. Anticipating serious trouble, Stanhope placed his men under arms on April 15, 1866. He prepared them to deploy at once should the mayor of Norfolk exercise his privilege under the Johnson policy to request military assistance.

On April 16, 1866, as eight hundred Black people marched toward Portsmouth, a white man fired a shot into their midst. The crowd charged and killed the man. Captain Stanhope sent an escort of infantry to protect the crowd and escorted them safely home. Later, learning that whites in Norfolk were preparing a reprisal against the Black settlement, Stanhope consulted with the mayor. The mayor lamented that his meager, unsympathetic, and unreliable all-white police force could not protect the Black people and pleaded with the officer to use troops for that purpose. Presumably acting under President Johnson's policy that military commanders in the seceded states, on request, aid their civilian counterparts, Stanhope agreed to help.

At approximately 9:30 p.m., about one hundred men, armed and dressed in Confederate gray, assembled at the United Service Engine Fire House and proceeded to march. On spotting

Captain Stanhope and himself, who had been inspecting the area, the men in gray wheeled around from column to line and fired a volley of fifty shots toward the startled pair. After galloping back to headquarters, Stanhope ordered a lieutenant to take a company in search of his assailants or any other rioters and break them up. The soldiers were to hold their fire, but if fired upon, they were to respond both with bullets and fixed bayonets. When the company returned without having located the captain's attackers, Stanhope concluded that he must be dealing with an organized body of well-armed men. They could appear on signals, march in cadence, fire volleys, and disappear at will.

In a report to his superior headquarters, the Department of Virginia, Captain Stanhope recommended that both Norfolk and Portsmouth go under martial law. The city authorities are powerless to quell disturbances of any magnitude and are incredibly hostile to the Black population. While awaiting a reply, the captain requested and received support from a company of Marines sent by the commander of the Norfolk Navy Yard. He arranged with the local ferryboat company to operate late to transport reinforcements from Fort Monroe. Throughout the night of April 16, 1866, Stanhope's men and marines patrolled the streets of Norfolk. Still, they encountered no resistance stronger than occasional brickbats and sporadic sniper fire.

On April 17, 1866, Captain Stanhope heard that white rioters were organizing for an assault later that day to crush his command and exterminate the Black settlement. Anticipating the worst, Stanhope telegraphed Fort Monroe for reinforcement, and the post commander sent two hundred soldiers to Norfolk. The men arrived at dusk. Stanhope ordered the mayor to announce publicly that the Army would crush any attempt at rioting that evening. All rioting had ceased by the evening of April 17.

Over Johnson's veto, Congress passed the Civil Rights Act of April 9, 1866, and wrote the Fourteenth Amendment to the Constitution. The Act was designed to protect Black Americans from restrictive legislation, and the Freedmen's Bureau Bill of July 16, 1866, extended the agency's life. Both passed over Johnson's veto. Doubts about the constitutionality of the Acts led the radicals to incorporate most of their provisions later.

In early 1866, Congressional Republicans, appalled by the pogrom's mass killing of formerly enslaved people and the adoption of the restrictive Vagrancy Act, seized control of Reconstruction from President Johnson. Congress denied representatives from the former Confederate states their seats in the House of Representatives. The act was passed, and an amendment to the Constitution was written, extending citizenship rights to Black Americans and guaranteeing them equal protection under the law.

The amendment committed to the abolition of enslavement and the establishment of civil rights for newly freed Black Americans. It also reduced representation in Congress of any former Confederate state that had deprived Black Americans of the vote. The Congress sent the proposed Fourteenth Amendment to the states for ratification. Still, it did not include any representatives or senators from former Confederate states.

This exclusion ensured that the amendment, designed to guarantee equal protection and due process under the law, would be shaped by the perspectives of those loyal to the Federal Government.

In 1867, Congress overrode a presidential veto to pass an act that divided the South into military districts. This act placed the former Confederate states under martial law pending their adoption of constitutions guaranteeing civil liberties to former enslaved people. The Reconstruction Act of 1867 gave Black American men in the South the right to vote three years before ratification of the amendment. With the vote came representation.

Although the law empowered him to remove recalcitrant former Confederate states officeholders, President Johnson refused. He also forbade the Army from trying violations of federal law in its courts or from prohibiting activities that were not specifically in violation of federal or local statutes. Many Republicans regarded the President's actions as a systematic effort to thwart the will of Congress and lend aid and comfort to enemies of the federal Government. The hot-tempered Johnson labeled the Republicans scoundrels in the treasonous tradition of Benedict Arnold.

To prevent the President from obstructing its Reconstruction program, Congress passed several laws restricting presidential powers. These laws prevented him from appointing justices to the Supreme Court and restricted his authority over the Army. The Tenure of Office Act prevented him from removing officeholders appointed with Senate consent without Senate approval.

In August 1867, Johnson tested the Tenure of Office Act by removing Secretary of War Edwin Stanton. This act prompted Republicans in Congress to impeach and remove the President.

Freedmen served in Virginia legislature for the first time in 1869. One of the first acts of the new General Assembly was to ratify the Fifteenth Amendment to the Constitution. It prohibits any state from denying any man the right to vote because of his race, color, or previous condition of servitude. Despite their legal political equality, many white Americans continued to treat Black Americans as lesser citizens, both literally and figuratively.

Black political leaders in the years following the Civil War tended to be somewhat wealthier and more educated than other Black citizens of Virginia. They faced many of the same difficulties and obstacles as the men who were born into slavery. They worked in jobs similar to those of other freedmen, such as mechanics, farmers, or ministers. These pioneering Black American political leaders in Virginia and throughout the South utilized the guarantee of suffrage in the Fifteenth Amendment to their full advantage, paving the way for future leaders to follow in their footsteps.

Some of them were born free, such as William Gilliam of Prince George's County, Peter K. Jones of Greenville County, and William H. Patterson of Charles City County. Other members of the assembly in 1871–1872 were born into slavery.

Among them were Richard G. L. Paige of Norfolk, Peter Jacob Carter of Northampton County, Joseph P. Evans of Petersburg, and Henry Turpin of Goochland County. Before becoming involved in politics, Paige was educated at Howard University, and Carter served in the United States Army and later attended what is now Hampton University.

Other Black American political leaders were lawyers, storekeepers, and postmasters, which helped them become well known throughout their communities. Henry Cox of Powhatan County may have also been born free.

In February 1867, Congress approved the First Reconstruction Act. The act introduced the concept of Congressional Reconstruction, although two additional acts supplemented it. Andrew Johnson vetoed all three Reconstruction Acts, but a congressional majority overrode his veto.

Johnson's policy of Reconstruction did not require Confederate states to guarantee voting rights for Black men or involve Black people in the writing of new state constitutions. By 1867, Congress had grown frustrated that former Confederate leaders were controlling former Confederate state governments and actively working to undermine Emancipation and the Reconstruction Amendments.

In March 1867, Congress overrode President Johnson's veto, and the First Reconstruction Act became law. The act implemented restoration to the United States as a long-term post-war transition that empowered Black men as an electorate and excluded former government officials who had aided the Confederacy. It divided the former Confederate states into five Reconstruction districts held under federal military control and led by commanding generals.

Each state had to complete a series of requirements to earn full federal restoration. The first was to hold a state convention of elected delegates and draft a new constitution establishing voting rights for men of all races. To earn complete restoration to the United States, these states had to write new constitutions and have them ratified by a majority of voters. Further, the states had to elect new officials under the new constitutional guidelines, ratify the amendments to the United States Constitution, and secure reinstatement from Congress.

As Reconstruction continued, violent white resistance to Black political power, citizenship rights, and freedom extended to pogroms throughout the South. It diminished Black electoral influence and restored to office many former Confederate officials who still promoted white supremacist policies. Even with the protection of federal troops and the force of federal law, Black people empowered to participate in the remaking of the South faced violence at the hands of resentful white mobs.

On March 2, 1867, Congress passed the Reconstruction Act over President Johnson's veto. Pending the former Confederate states' adoption of constitutions guaranteeing civil liberties to formerly enslaved people, Congress passed the Reconstruction Act on March 2, 1867, over President Johnson's veto. Also known as the Military Reconstruction Act of 1867, its primary purpose was to establish a systematic method for enforcing United States laws. The act also ensured that readmitted former Confederate states aligned with the nation's values.

In January 1866, the Senate presented the first federal civil rights bill in American history. Designed as part of a Republican legislative program, it shored up the objectives of the Freedmen's Bureau Bill. It implemented the intentions of the Thirteenth Amendment. The act formally equated the rights of freed people with those of citizens. It provided for the federal protection of those rights.

The act provided federal protection to all Americans—regardless of race or previous condition of servitude—against the assaults of both state and private action. These protections were necessary in the face of racist laws, which severely restricted and regulated the personal, civil, and labor rights of Black Americans living in the former enslave holding states. The rights guaranteed and protected by the act included those targeted by the racist laws. In particular, the rights to make and enforce contracts, own and sell property, sue and participate in legal cases, and benefit from all laws protecting the security of persons and property.

The Reconstruction Act imposed military rule on the former Confederate states until new state governments were established. It divided the South into five military districts and placed the former Confederate states under martial law. Despite the presence of federal troops and the backing of Congressional law, Black settlements actively participating in the political end of enslavement in the United States still faced brutal violence from aggressive white mobs. The Reconstruction Act designated Virginia Military District One.

The act also limited some former Confederate officials and military officers' rights to vote and to run for public office. Meanwhile, the Reconstruction Acts gave formerly enslaved men the right to vote and hold public office. After their service in Texas, the USCT Regiments were assigned to the Military District One, which encompassed Virginia. Although Black soldiers continued to face discrimination during their time of service, they demonstrated bravery, valor, and dedication in the face of adversity. Many USCT regiments stayed in service after the Federal Army demobilization. Black regiments made up as much as one-third of the Federal forces occupying the former Confederate states.

Reconstruction civil-military duty presented rewards and challenges. On the one hand, Black soldiers could play an active role in supporting the Freedmen's Bureau, protecting formerly enslaved people, and enforcing the Reconstruction amendments. On the other hand, they faced hostility from white southern civilians, and they had to deal with a government whose commitment to protecting Black people wavered.

After leaving the Federal armies, a future of both possibilities and prejudice confronted Black soldiers. Racism and discrimination resulted in ongoing oppression for Black people in the United States. However, many individual members of the

USCT found that their military service had earned them trust and respect, at least within the Black settlements.

Parson stated that many Black veterans established careers in politics during the Reconstruction era. At least forty Black delegates to the former Confederate state's constitutional conventions had served in the USCT, and many more Black veterans won elections to state legislatures and to Congress.

After duty on the Rio Grande, the 1st USCT Regiment mustered out on February 4, 1866. Parson returned to Virginia, a free man, the weight of injustice lifting; the familiar scent of saltwater beaches and damp earth filled his lungs. His new orders, a crisp sheet of paper, felt reassuring in his assignment with the Military District One, Fort Monroe. The distant sounds of the Chesapeake Bay hinted at a new life, a new beginning.

Parson returned to Virginia and learned that while Black people argued for the right to vote, many white Virginians could not vote because they had supported the Confederacy. Still, the federal Government required men who had supported the Confederacy to take an oath of allegiance to the United States or obtain a presidential pardon before they could regain their suffrage.

Early in 1865, even before the Civil War was over, Black people in Norfolk began discussing the legal and political implications of the abolition of enslavement and the end of military protection. The right to vote was certainly on their agenda.

Parson met with the men who founded the Colored Monitor Union Club to seek all the rights of citizenship. This includes "the right of universal suffrage to loyal men, without distinction of color, and to memorialize and allow colored citizens equal franchise rights with other citizens. Parson explained his role at Fort Monroe. He described how they cooperated with the Freedmen's Bureau and helped with education, employment, and the overall transition of formerly enslaved people into society. The men met again later and agreed to cooperate, organizing in other settlements.

Parson's insight into enslavement and the Army allowed him to understand and express empathy. He then shared his experiences and how he learned to accept the limitations of self-liberation. Instead of complaining, he suggested making the best of one's limitations and living a life of resistance and tolerance. Recognizing his limitations empowered Parson, as he ignored external restrictions and used them to discover his strengths.

Following the war, USCT units from the Army of the James performed civil-military duty in Virginia, with the last regiments mustered out in February 1866. The XXV Corps mustered out of service in January 1866. After the Civil War ended and the abolition of enslavement, Parson believed freedom was much more than just the absence of enslavement.

With wisdom and urgency, Congress passed the First Reconstruction Act, which split the former Confederate states into military zones. The challenge of restoring the Union was enormous, requiring the readmission of the former Confederate states, the establishment of loyal governments, and integrating the formerly enslaved people into society. The Congress passed the Civil Rights Act over Johnson's veto.

Parson's quest for human and civil rights elicited strong emotional responses. Parson anticipated that the Reconstruction's outcome would overthrow the status quo and replace it with freedom, citizenship, and equality. The hopes, fears, joys, sorrows, pain, and tears of enslavement gave way to a series of events. They led Black people into a vastly different life from the one they had just left behind. Parson's insights taught him that people are individuals, not subordinate members of humanity. They have a right to pursue life, liberty, and happiness, and should not sacrifice themselves for others. He believed that they require freedom to do this and must not be the property of another person.

After the suspension of open war hostilities, insurgent groups emerged with the expressed purpose of suppressing Black and white Republicans from voting and gradually diminishing their power. The bitterness caused by the Civil War lingered, and most of the former Confederacy sympathizers strongly opposed the freed people's new position in society.

In summary, the Congressional Reconstruction movement confronted the defeated former Confederacy in a state of devastation. The old social and economic order, founded on enslavement, completely collapsed, leaving a void in its wake.

CHAPTER FIVE

Parson Back Home on Furlough

Parson's boots crunched over the gravel at Fort Monroe, the sound sharp in the chilly morning air. He had been away from the fort for weeks, but it never truly felt like home—not the way Southampton did, not the way the woods near his mother's old garden smelled after rain. The Army had given him a uniform, a rifle, and a purpose. But every time he crossed through the gates, he felt the same old ache—a longing, tangled with dread, for the land and people that shaped him.

His hands trembled as he paused at the sentry post, waiting for the young white corporal to scan his leave papers. Parson tried to still his breath, to hide the nerves. He had faced down Confederates at Petersburg, seen men fall screaming in the mud. But the fear that crept up his spine now was quieter, heavier. He was returning home to Virginia, a state torn open by war, where the promise of freedom still tasted like ash in too many mouths.

Inside Headquarters, the mood was tense. Men shuffled through, some laughing loudly to cover their nerves, others hunched over desks, writing letters home. Parson signed in, his name one among hundreds. But for the Black people of Virginia, this place was everything. It was the seat of Federal power, the only thing standing between them and the mobs, the laws, the old masters who wanted things the way they had always been. When freedmen and their families arrived at the gates, hungry, scared, or beaten, it was soldiers like Parson who took their statements, wrote their affidavits, and tried to promise some measure of safety.

Morale was always in short supply, so the Army issued furloughs—brief windows of time when a man could disappear back into his old life. Parson welcomed the chance, though he did not fool himself. Virginia was no safer now than in the worst days of the war. The First Reconstruction Act had been signed, and suddenly it felt like the whole South was on fire again. White resistance was not a whisper anymore; it was a roar. Reports came in daily—lynchings, arson, men in hoods riding at night. The new laws said Black men could vote, could hold office, and could finally be citizens. But the old powers fought back with everything they had, their rage and fear spilling into the streets.

His commander, a stern man with a tired face, gathered the soldiers just before roll call. "There's anger out there," he said, voice flat. "You'll see it in every glance, every word. They think we're the enemy. They think these new laws are an insult. Be careful. Watch your backs."

Parson listened, jaw clenched. He had known hatred before. But this was different—a raw, organized resistance, determined to erase every inch of progress. Troops were stationed in every county and town, but it was never enough. For every patrol that broke up a gathering of night riders, two more sprang up down the road. Black families, newly freed, were hunted in their own homes. Even the most minor victories were shadowed by violence. Parson's own detachment had lost two men last month, ambushed on a lonely road outside Emporia. The news spread fast. No one needed reminding that the war was not truly over.

He had seen the cost of this new peace. A woman, her hair streaked with gray, holding her wounded boy on the steps of the Bureau office. A preacher, trembling as he described the night a mob burned his church to the ground. Parson had learned to swallow his anger, to offer a steady voice and a sympathetic ear. But inside, the frustration grew. How could freedom mean so little?

Virginia was supposed to be rejoining the Union, building loyal governments, and learning to live up to the promise of the flag again. But everywhere Parson looked, the old order clawed its way back. Federal troops could enforce the law, could help Black men vote, testify, and claim their rights. But white supremacists slipped back into office, their power undiminished. They wore new faces, but the hatred was the same. Sometimes Parson wondered if any of it really mattered, if the struggle was worth it. But then he would remember his mother's voice, the way she had whispered hope in the darkest nights, and he'd push on.

There were moments—brief, shining moments—when things felt possible. On the outskirts of town, in settlements built by freedmen, you could see it. Black men and women, heads held high, opening schools in battered shacks, starting churches, forming families. The Army had never cared about public education before. Now, they help fund schools, hand out books, and feed hungry children. Parson walked the dirt lanes of these settlements, sometimes welcomed, sometimes eyed with suspicion. He saw the spark in young eyes, the pride in elders who had survived too much. It made the danger worth it.

But the countryside was a battleground. The Army rooted out old Confederates, took over local government, and replaced judges and sheriffs with men who swore loyalty to the Union. Sometimes it worked. Sometimes the old powers simply waited, biding their time, plotting revenge. Parson remembered the siege at Petersburg, how every day brought a new wave of suicides, men broken by loss and desperation. His own body remembered, too—tight muscles, sleepless nights, a heart that would not slow down.

The Freedmen's Bureau did what it could. In the Jerusalem courthouse in Southampton, agents worked day and night to feed the hungry, treat the sick, and negotiate contracts between former masters and their laborers. But the work was never done. Parson watched the agents struggle—short on supplies, battered by endless complaints, caught between white anger and Black desperation. Still, they pressed on. The schools they built, the families they reunited, and the legal help they offered — these things mattered. Parson saw it every day in the faces of his people.

Solomon and Louisa, Parson's parents, lived now on an abandoned patch of land near Jacob's farm. They had made a home out of ruins, planting a garden, building a rough fence, and sharing what little they had with neighbors. Under military rule, they had a shot—just a shot—at something like stability. Parson clung to that hope, even as he saw how fragile it was.

He took pride in his work, but he was not naïve. Proclamations and amendments did not change hearts overnight. Even with Jefferson Davis locked away and the Bureau spread across the countryside, freedom was a daily struggle. Black settlements lived under constant threat. It was Parson's job to defend them, but he knew he could not be everywhere at once. Each time a farm burned, or a family vanished in the night, he felt the failure keenly.

The Reconstruction Acts demanded a new way of living. Freedmen and their former enslavers were forced to face each other, to negotiate contracts, to share space in a world that no longer had clear lines. The Bureau set up special courts to settle disputes—sometimes it worked, sometimes it just delayed the violence. Parson watched his people try to build lives: opening businesses, attending church, searching for lost relatives. He believed in self-reliance, in the power of community. But he saw, too, how the weight of white anger and institutional hatred could crush even the strongest spirit.

His own understanding of freedom changed in these years. As a boy, he had dreamed of liberty as something bright and simple. Now, he saw the cracks. Freedom could be mocked, denied, twisted into something ugly. The insults, the violence, the laws designed to keep Black people down—all of it revealed just how fragile humanity could be. Parson learned to balance hope and realism, to fight for what he could, to mourn what he could not save.

Still, he insisted that peace had brought him a kind of independence he had never known before. Even as new laws passed to keep Black people from renting land, owning guns, or sending their children to school—even as old masters tried to claim apprenticeships for children who should have been free— he held on. He watched the Bureau agents feed both Black and white families, saw the resentment in some faces, the gratitude in others. He listened to his father talk about dignity, about refusing to bow even when the odds were stacked against them.

Parson's own transformation was slow, shaped by every injustice he witnessed. Legal freedom was just the first step. Every job denied, every house refused, every unfair trial reminded him how far they still had to go. He came to believe that the government had a duty to protect Black people, to enforce the rights they had been promised. These convictions took root in him, quiet but unshakable.

He never forgot the day a detachment of U.S. Colored Troops marched through a Black settlement. Children ran alongside the soldiers, laughing, begging for scraps. Mothers wept openly, waving handkerchiefs. The Army brought food and news, hope and reassurance. White townsfolk stood apart, stone-faced, arms crossed. But for a few hours, the settlement felt alive—a place where dreams seemed possible again.

When Parson was finally granted his furlough, he packed his kit with methodical care. He left his rifle and Army gear behind, carrying only his papers and a change of clothes. He was eager to see his parents, to hold Frances, his sweet-faced girl, to walk the familiar paths of home. But he also knew the dangers waited—white men who resented his uniform, neighbors who had not forgiven his family's escape from slavery, laws that could snare him for the smallest offense.

His first stop was the Freedmen's Bureau office at the Jerusalem courthouse. The place was crowded, voices echoing off the cracked plaster walls. Parson waited his turn, listening to veterans ask about pensions, mothers plead for lost children, and old men beg for land. When his turn came, he spoke with an agent about veterans' benefits, about education, employment, and property. The answers were never simple—money was scarce, the future uncertain. But the agent listened, took notes, and promised to do what he could.

Parson learned that the Bureau had helped his father, Solomon, negotiate a labor contract with Jacob. The terms were better than nothing, but the scales still tipped toward the white landowner. Solomon now worked for a fixed wage, not as a sharecropper, but it was a hard bargain. Land, tools, autonomy— these were still out of reach.

He met with Jacob, the man who'd once owned him. The conversation was awkward, measured. Jacob wanted the old hands back—Solomon, Henry, Joseph. He needed them to keep the farm running. Parson agreed to the terms but made it clear: things had changed. He would work, but he would not be owned.

They planned for his return after his discharge, sketching out the coming months in careful, cautious words.

Most Black people in Southampton owned nothing but the clothes on their backs. They had to bargain for work on white farms, face to face with men who'd once claimed them as property. Some landowners tried to revive the old gang-labor system, but the Bureau kept a close watch. Abuse was common, but not as unchecked as before.

Then came the Virginia Vagrancy Act of 1866—a law designed to shackle Black freedom. Under provisional governor Pierpont, the legislature passed restrictions meant to control labor and reinforce white supremacy. Black people could be charged as "vagrants" for being jobless or homeless, then forced into hard labor, chained together. The law banned Black people from voting, owning guns, gathering in public, or even testifying in court. Petty crimes led to long sentences, all to keep Black labor cheap and compliant.

Parson saw the effects every day. Men were arrested for refusing to sign labor contracts, families were fined for traveling without papers, and children were forced into apprenticeships. The law punished poverty, not crime. Landowners like Jacob used it to fill their fields, to keep wages low and discipline high. Other laws restricted Black business, property, and even movement.

The Vagrancy Act infuriated Federal officials and helped push the nation toward Congressional Reconstruction, with new amendments and military rule in the South. Black people fought back, challenging arrests, refusing to accept second-class status.

Federal loyalists began questioning President Johnson's policies, wondering if anything short of direct intervention could work.

For Parson, the fight was personal. Every day, he looked at his hands—once scarred by the lash, now callused from hard work—and wondered how much had really changed. He walked the line between hope and despair, trying to build a life for himself and his loved ones, trying to believe in a future that sometimes seemed impossibly far away.

Yet even in the darkest moments, he held on. Home was still home—the scent of pine, the sound of his mother's laughter, the touch of Frances' hand in his. He was free, and he would never let the world forget it.

During his civil-military duties in District One, Parson witnessed postwar Reconstruction and demobilization. As the postwar demobilization period progressed, the number of federal Army positions in the former Confederacy steadily declined. This reduction in the size of forces following the Civil War contributed to a collapse of law and order. Consequently, the insufficient size of forces played a role in weakening the protection for Black citizens and white loyalists from the violence perpetrated by white insurgents opposing Reconstruction.

Parson had obtained vital intelligence about the humanitarian and aid missions in the area. He discovered that half of the occupation force consisted of USCT regiments. These regiments joined the Union Army later in the conflict. He discussed hate organizations emerging to harass, intimidate, and even murder Black individuals and white sympathizers. These groups were Confederate sympathizers or outlaws, and their crimes were racially motivated.

By the end of 1865, armed white men, some with blackened faces and calling themselves Regulators, had appeared in remote parts of Virginia. The regulators were former Confederate veterans who were members of the KKK. They used similar terror tactics against freed Black people, including theft, arson, and murder, to advance their racist ideology. Their unrestrained aggression against Black people rapidly intensified. To keep peace and order in the former Confederate states, Radical Republicans believed a military presence was required.

As Parson noted, after the Radical Republicans won control of Congress, most Republicans sought to safeguard Black Americans through legislation, despite President Johnson's strong objections. They overrode a presidential veto to enact a Civil Rights law in April 1866, followed by a revised Freedmen's Bureau measure two months later. The actions of Congress fueled the increasing anger. The Radical Republicans saw the perpetuation of inequality and racial hatred as intolerable. On civil-military operations duty at Fort Monroe, Parson witnessed the emergence of an unsettling era of peace amid the war-torn terrain of Reconstruction.

As the implementation of the Reconstruction Act of 1867 progressed, violent resistance from white insurgents intensified. This resistance targeted Black political authority, equality, citizenship, rights, and freedom. When Johnson took office, he continued President Lincoln's conceptual plan. This strategy did not provide voting rights for Black men in the former Confederate states. It also excluded Black people from the formulation of new state constitutions. This instilled dread throughout the South and reduced Black electoral influence. Many former Confederate politicians returned to politics, continuing to promote white nationalist policies.

Major General Howard was committed to keeping freed people safe from harm and guaranteeing equitable access to the law. As Parson mentioned, he strove to build schools for them. For the first time, Black people could openly read, write, refuse to work for their former owners, travel freely, and reunite with their families. They traveled often, hoping to find husbands, wives, children, and other relatives. As individuals and families, and as members of churches and mutual aid societies, formerly enslaved people worked hard to make their freedom meaningful.

Parson believed that the Reconstruction Act of 1867 promised Black men the right to vote while excluding former Confederate officials. The Act required that each former Confederate state meet specific federal restoration standards. First, they needed to assemble elected delegates to create a new constitution. This new constitution had to grant voting rights to men of all races.

The election ushered in a new phase of Reconstruction aimed at protecting Black voting rights and establishing integrated governments in the seceded states. It intensified the violent resistance from white Confederacy sympathizers and insurgent groups. This resistance, fueled by a desire to maintain white supremacy and regain political control, manifested in various forms of pogrom directed at Black Americans.

In the former Confederate states, Black men organized Equal Rights Leagues to advocate for equal rights and citizenship. According to Parson, they conducted local, state, and national assemblies to protest unfair treatment by the Army, governmental officials, and companies. Among the key organizers were men who had held leadership positions both before and during the regular wartime hostilities. These men campaigned for guaranteed rights and contested discriminatory policies. The leagues, especially the National Equal Rights League formed by Frederick Douglass, are considered forerunners of the twentieth-century civil rights movement.

On June 13, 1866, Congress proposed the Fourteenth Amendment. This Amendment granted citizenship and equal protection under the law to all persons born or naturalized in the United States, regardless of race, color, or previous condition of servitude. Furthermore, it restricted office-holding for those who had participated in the rebellion. However, the former Confederate states refused to ratify the Amendment. Congress established the Reconstruction Act of 1867 in response to the former Confederate states' refusal to ratify the Amendment, which guaranteed civil rights to Black people.

This Act created military authority in the South and required new state constitutions to include provisions for Black suffrage. The primary goal was to protect the rights of formerly enslaved people and ensure their participation in American politics.

To be fully restored to the Union, the former Confederate states had to create new constitutions that would be ratified by most of their populations before new leaders could be elected. Under the new constitutional principles, the former Confederate states were required to approve the Amendment to the United States Constitution and obtain congressional approval.

Despite the presence of federal troops and the force of federal law, Black delegates empowered to participate in the Reconstruction of the South were subjected to violence from enraged white mobs. In 1865, the right to vote heralded sweeping changes in Black priorities, calling for the protection and enforcement of their civil rights in the United States, particularly in Virginia. Enfranchisement enabled them to pursue broader goals, such as political representation and social justice.

As Parson noted, before 1865, the federal law restricted voting to adult white men. The right to vote was central to his agenda, as he continually promoted civil rights, free public education, and Black land ownership. Even before the regular fighting in the conflict ended in 1865, Black people in Norfolk began discussing the legal and political implications of the abolition of enslavement and the end of military protection.

In February 1865, white residents of Norfolk, who had remained loyal to the Union, proposed restoring the civilian municipal government. Simultaneously, Black residents petitioned the President and the commander of District One, requesting that any replacement of the existing military government with a civilian one be established only on a loyal and equal basis. They held marches and submitted petitions calling for the protection and enforcement of their civil rights. They emphasized that the Thirteenth Amendment alone was insufficient without accompanying legislation guaranteeing equality before the law.

Tensions between Black people and whites boiled over in Norfolk on April 16, 1866, when a parade of Black Americans celebrated Congress's passage of a national Civil Rights Act. The demonstrators carried banners for fraternal and political societies. Some white people threw rocks and bricks at the parade, and a fight between marchers and a city police officer began after the accidental discharge of a gun.

Violence continued through the night as armed bands of whites attacked Black people, killing two and injuring several others. United States troops declared martial law to control the mobs. As Parson recalled the pogrom he witnessed, violent vigilantes beat and massacred Black residents of Norfolk. Civilian authorities were reluctant to quell disturbances of any magnitude and were extremely hostile to the Black population.

The political and racial violence horrified the Congressional Republican members who supported Black people. Following the 1866 elections, the Radical Republicans gained complete control over congressional decision-making, securing control of both the House of Representatives and the

Senate. This gave them sufficient power to override any potential vetoes by President Johnson.

While home on furlough, Parson learned that the Freedmen's Bureau, led by Major J. H. Putnam, negotiated and enforced labor contracts in Southampton County. One of the crucial tasks of the Freedmen's Bureau was to assist unskilled freed people in Southampton County in finding gainful employment. Major Putnam sent detachments across the countryside to gather information on Black Americans, including their names, addresses, and occupations. Emancipation led many enslaved Black people to flee to the Union-controlled area across the Blackwater River. This led to the creation of a new labor dynamic in postwar Virginia.

Former enslavers no longer controlled the labor of formerly enslaved people, and the people gained some but not complete control over their labor. Putnam cheerfully reported, "Able-bodied Negroes can very readily find employment at fair wages." Major Putnam received numerous applications for laborers. Those who were unemployed were readily provided with opportunities. Putnam also took an optimistic view of local agricultural prospects.

Parson made different assessments of the situation. Sounding like an expert cavalry scout, he reported that Southampton's formerly enslaved people no longer worked like enslaved laborers. Many left the scene of their former bondage and fled to urban areas. Some moved from the county to work in factories, on the docks, and on farms redistributed by the

Bureau. Others remained in the county wherever they found a vacant house; they moved into the abandoned property, uncertain of their futures.

The former Confederates sought to bind formerly enslaved laborers to a particular landowner for an entire season, with both the power of law and the threat of coercion to enforce the new arrangements. Clinging to their prejudices, they insisted that Black laborers could only become productive under the control of white landowners. Believing formerly enslaved people were naturally inclined to self-indulgence and lacked foresight, they urged Putnam to grant them significant control over Black laborers' supervision and discipline.

Putnam assisted freed people in negotiating labor contracts and also helped to enforce them, sometimes stepping in to protect their rights in court. The agency labor agreements took many forms. Some details on who would be employed and their wages. Parson found that these contracts used the exact phrasing, implying that Bureau agents frequently participated in labor agreement talks.

Back in Southampton County, Parson observed the cotton fields shimmering in the sun, with freshly plowed rows that emitted the earthy scent of turned soil. He noted how sharecropping, a system etched in the weary sighs of laborers and the creak of rusty plows, emerged as the primary form of farm labor in Virginia. Sharecropping provided Black people with some degree of control over their work and lives. In theory, it freed them from the gang-labor system of enslavement.

However, it often left them in debt. Sharecroppers usually owed landowners more for tools and supplies than they could repay.

Parson described sharecropping as a system where Black families rented small plots of land from landowners. In return, they gave part of their crop to the landowner each year. Although sharecropping had existed for centuries, in Military District One, it primarily served to burden formerly enslaved people financially. This made their limited control feel pointless. While abolitionists fought to end enslavement before the war, they missed the actual struggles that formerly enslaved people faced in finding freedom in a new society.

Parson learned that Solomon and other formerly enslaved people in Southampton hoped to buy small plots of land and become landowners themselves. Instead, they had to make binding agreements with Jacob, their former owner. When their hopes for land ownership grew, they pushed for new rules to govern employer-employee relationships. Solomon wanted to own a store to sell the extra food he grew. However, segregation and discrimination made it tough for Black people to own businesses.

After enslavement ended and the economy was devastated by the war, a different conflict arose during Reconstruction between many white landowners and freed Black people. They disagreed on how to create a paid labor force and provide opportunities for employment and economic independence. The Freedmen's Bureau played a crucial role in shaping labor relations between newly emancipated Black Americans and their former enslavers. To ease the conflict, the

Bureau helped draft and supervise employer-employee contracts to protect the rights of freed Black people.

To assist the newly freed Black population in Southampton County, the military established settlements for them in towns bordering Jerusalem. Concurrently, the Bureau Agents provided humanitarian aid and implemented the Butler labor system.

In the effort to help the freed Black people in Southampton County, the military settled them in towns on the fringes of Jerusalem. The northern missionaries started running schools in the military district only because they were asked to do so. Buildings were accessible to the teachers, as they had been left vacant by white people. Buildings were not available for use in towns where the military officials did not want them to be available.

Beyond immediate relief, the Freedmen's Bureau also became involved in shaping labor relations in Southampton County. The district's local agents aided freedpeople in establishing and enforcing labor agreements in the new free labor market and, sometimes, intervened in court cases to protect their rights. Agents acted as judges to settle disputes over labor contracts. The agreements could also be enforced in local courts, and sometimes Bureau agents appeared as witnesses to verify or testify about the terms of labor contracts.

The contract between Solomon and Jacob included a provision that allowed the parties to appeal to the agency to annul the labor contract. Parson learned that Labor agreements took many forms. Some were basic contracts outlining pay rates and employment. Solomon and Jacob's agreement was exceptionally fair, giving either side the power to alter the contract monthly. That so many were involved implies that agents often took part in negotiating these labor contracts, serving as intermediaries or representatives for the newly freed workers and securing some fairness in the contract conditions.

Returning home after deployment was a joyous occasion, but Parson faced enormous challenges on Jacob's land. He found his family living in a Black settlement outside Jerusalem Township. This cabin was a two-room wooden structure with a porch and a tin roof. The family lived close together, using the porch for storage, washing, and even iceboxes. The main room served as a kitchen, living space, and sleeping area, with beds often shared among family members. Their cabin was a refuge, a symbol of family solidarity.

While gathered in the cabin, Solomon and Louisa told Parson about the new county laws. While he was away, the county enacted discriminatory laws to restrict the freedoms of formerly enslaved people. Schools, churches, restaurants, hotels, public transport, restrooms, and water fountains were labeled "white only" or "colored." These signs highlighted racial inequality and the oppression of Black Americans.

Despite this, Solomon and Louisa sought the assistance of the Military District. They wanted to own land rather than work for Jacob. They tried to avoid supervision and harsh treatment. They asked Parson if the Union Army planned to develop 40-acre tracts of abandoned land. Black residents in

Southampton County hoped to acquire confiscated property and break up large estates.

They understood the Confiscation Act of 1862, which allowed the Federal government to seize the property of Confederate officials and supporters. This included land and other assets. Parson explained that seizing property required court proceedings, which could be long and complex. During Reconstruction, President Johnson undermined the loosely enforced Acts.

Black citizens, newly freed yet still oppressed, faced ridicule and violence from white mobs. The Bureau failed to protect and enforce the civil rights of Black Americans. Parson had to prepare for the prejudice that hindered his self-liberation. In public, he avoided excessive talk about his dangers and achievements. He knew that recounting his experiences might be enjoyable for him, but not for others.

They also shared stories of violent vigilantes who attacked Parson's allies. Civilian authorities were reluctant to stop the violence and were often hostile to Black people. Many falsely believed that whites lynched Black men for allegedly raping white women. However, most historical accounts showed a lack of credible accusations. During Parson's life, no white person was punished for participating in lynchings.

Racial ridicule and violence grew after Emancipation as Black people demanded full citizenship, including voting rights. Poor and working-class whites felt squeezed politically and economically, so they turned to minstrelsy. This distorted the culture of Black people, depicting them as irresponsible and laughable. Minstrel performances painted Black people as lazy, ignorant, and prone to crime. These stereotypes made civil rights efforts more difficult. Racial stereotypes made it easier for whites to deny Black people their full rights without recognizing individual differences.

White mobs committed brutal lynchings, instilling fear in Black settlements. They hanged Black men from trees, leaving a stench of injustice and helplessness. Across the country, stereotypes fueled violence, enforcing segregation and maintaining control over Black people. Mobs hanged, burned, or brutally murdered Black individuals like a pogrom.

During the initial stages of Reconstruction, the government employed military officials to accomplish its post-war objectives. Constant irregular gunfire and violence filled the counties. Military governors played a vital role in protecting the rights of freed people, but the era's politics and society limited their success. These goals proved unattainable through the former Confederate authorities. Congress may have ended the Bureau too soon. Still, it helped set terms for some planters and Black farm operators to build effective working relationships.

Back home on furlough, Parson witnessed the Federal government distributing food, building hospitals, providing medical aid, negotiating labor contracts for formerly enslaved people, and settling disputes. It also helped them legalize marriages, find lost relatives, and support Black veterans. Many Union veterans worked for the Bureau to assist formerly enslaved Black men and women. Parson wanted constitutionally guaranteed rights in Virginia, rejecting contracts that mandated group work.

Initially, Military District commanders also oversaw Freedmen's Bureau operations. Later, this responsibility came under the Bureau's commissioner. In Virginia, sharecropping became the central farming system. Black families rented small plots of land, paying the landowner a share of their crop each year. In Southampton County, white landowners made sharecropping agreements with Black families after the constitutional Amendment ended enslavement. Sharecropping became a common compromise.

Concurrently, the civil-military operations and the Freedmen's Bureau functioned as federal representatives in Virginia settlements. White terrorist groups mocked and attacked them for helping Black people. They saw this as interference. Despite granting formerly enslaved citizens their rights, the Federal government took little action to help them acquire the promised land.

CHAPTER SIX

The Civil Rights Act of 1866

Parson's boots hit the dust of Military District One with a heavy, familiar thud. The land was his, in that way a man claims soil he has walked and bled on, but nothing about the world felt familiar anymore. Soldiers drifted back in ragged clusters, blue coats faded, faces drawn, knowing that neither war nor peace could ever return what the past had stolen. For Parson, it was a homecoming that tasted of iron and uncertainty.

He saw, almost at once, that the end of the war had not ended the cruelty. In the shadows of half-burned cabins and among the twisted roots of old plantation oaks, men with power and old grudges found new ways to keep Black families pinned beneath their boots. They schemed to keep schools shuttered, to block every colored child's hand from turning a page, to lock the door to any land that could sustain hope or hunger. Some did it with laws, others with rope and torch, and the rest by simply looking away.

Southampton's sky was heavy with the memory of freedom just out of reach. Black families huddled in corners, always waiting for a night they might not survive. Emancipation, Parson realized, wasn't a sunrise but a long, uneven dawn — every new promise of liberty followed by another night of violence. In this county, the story of freedom was written in blood and silence, in dreams broken as soon as they were spoken aloud.

Congress, back in Washington, made speeches about freedom and equality, their words floating down the long road south like scraps of paper. The Reconstruction laws sounded hopeful enough, but Parson saw little of that hope in his neighbors' eyes. The men in charge could not agree on how to make freedom stick. For Southampton's freedmen, the years after war felt like waiting for rain in a drought, watching as every new law was choked by the weeds of hatred and indifference. They faced hunger, the grinding suspicion of white neighbors, and the threat of the Vagrancy Act — a law that could turn any Black man without work into a criminal overnight. Worst of all, there was the sense that no one in government cared enough to see what was happening, let alone stop it.

The first time Parson heard about the Civil Rights Act of 1866, it was almost as if someone had cracked open a window in a stifling room. The law meant Black men were citizens — citizens! — entitled to the same rights as any white man: the right to own land, to sign contracts, to speak for themselves in court. It sounded like a spell, a promise that the old world was truly gone. But Parson had seen too many promises wither in the sun. He watched as Southern lawmakers twisted the rules, inventing new ways to keep Black people poor and powerless, and he wondered if a law passed in Washington could ever really reach into the dirt of Southampton.

The Act overturned the Dred Scott decision — an old wound that said no Black man could ever be a citizen. Parson remembered the bitterness he had tasted the first time he had learned of that ruling, how it had knotted his insides with anger and shame. Now, the government said he belonged. But belonging, Parson thought, was more than a piece of paper. It was safety, a place to stand, the right way to wake up each morning, and know your family could stay together.

The Freedmen's Bureau was the government's hand in the South, and for a while, it felt like things might actually change. Parson watched as men he had grown up with — men who had once been bought and sold as property — lined up to vote, to organize, to build churches and schools. The Bureau's officers wore their uniforms with purpose, walking the muddy lanes of Southampton with clipboards and quiet authority, sometimes stopping to chat, sometimes settling disputes. It was not perfect. The white folks grumbled and plotted, and the old owners watched their former slaves with cold, calculating eyes. But for a moment, it seemed like the world might tip the other way.

Of course, nothing in the South changed without a fight. The word "Reconstruction" meant different things to different people. To some, it was about tearing down the old order, giving Black men the vote and a slice of land. To others, it was about patching things up just enough to keep the peace, then handing power right back to the same men who had started the war in the first place. Parson learned quickly that talk of freedom could get a man killed as surely as any battle.

The violence was never far away. Some nights, Parson heard gunshots in the distance, saw smoke rising from a neighbor's barn, or woke to find crude threats carved into fence posts. Black families lived in fear, not just of poverty but of sudden, senseless death. The men who had once worn gray uniforms now wore plain clothes, but their intent had not changed. They wanted Southampton back, just as it had been, with Black people on their knees and white men in charge.

Parson wore his blue coat with pride, the brass buttons catching the sunlight like small, stubborn stars. After all he had seen, he still believed in change. He stood taller now, shoulders squared by the weight of what he had survived. But everywhere he looked, the war's wounds were raw and open. The Thirteenth Amendment had ended slavery, but it had not brought peace. The promise of Reconstruction was tangled up in old grudges and new betrayals. Every day, Parson saw the cost of unfinished work — children turned away from school, men jailed for walking without a work permit, families torn apart by hunger and fear.

He thought about his own journey, the years spent fighting for a freedom that still slipped through his fingers. Integration, land redistribution, justice — these were words the newspapers used, but for Parson, they meant long, sleepless nights and hard choices. Reconstruction was a struggle, not just for the nation but for every man and woman trying to build a new life out of the ashes.

And yet, there were moments of sweetness. The air in Southampton was heavy with the scent of cherry blossoms, and sometimes, when the sun was low and the fields glowed gold, Parson let himself hope. He thought of Frances, the woman whose laughter had carried him through the worst of the war and imagined her pride when she saw him in uniform. He wanted her not just as a witness, but as a partner. He hoped she would see his struggle, understand it, and join him in the work — not out of duty, but out of belief in something better.

The end of the Civil War had not been the end of pain, but it had been an opening. Parson understood that the formal surrender of armies was just the beginning. Emancipation was a promise, not a gift. The Thirteenth Amendment had struck the chains, but it could not bind the hearts of men. The South was wounded — its fields ruined, its people bitter — and every attempt to build something new met fierce resistance.

In Southampton, the old ways died slowly. Freedom crept in, not with fanfare, but in quiet acts of courage. Parson and his brothers rebuilt their lives piece by piece. They started new churches, founded mutual aid societies, and tried to patch together families scattered by war. They opened small businesses, learned to read by firelight, and discovered the dignity in making choices for themselves. These were not political victories, but they were real and lasting — the change that grew from the ground up.

Parson's resolve deepened with each setback. Every injustice he witnessed fed his determination to push back, to keep learning and growing, even when the world seemed intent on shrinking him down. He worked with Lieutenant Deacon and the Bureau, helping neighbors file for citizenship, track down missing relatives, or claim land that rightfully belonged to them. It was exhausting, sometimes thankless work, but Parson saw it as a kind of self-liberation — a daily battle for dignity and progress.

His body bore the marks of struggle, but his mind was sharper than ever. The way he planned and the care he took with every detail showed a man remaking himself for a new world. He kept a careful schedule, balancing advocacy, farming, and the sacred duty of voting. He believed that every small victory — every field planted, every ballot cast — was another step down the road to true deliverance.

When the War Department started demobilizing the USCT regiments in 1866, Parson braced himself for disappointment. The process was slow, unfair, and laced with humiliation. White officers could resign at will, but Black enlisted men waited months for the Army's blessing. Parson and his brothers had enlisted in the 1st Cavalry Regiment, USCT, back in 1864, and they served faithfully until well into 1867. Their service was honorable, but the waiting gnawed at them. They worried about families left behind in Southampton, about the crops that needed tending and the children who asked each day when their fathers would return.

The Army paid Black and white soldiers the same in theory, but in practice, the wait for paychecks was endless. Parson's mood soured as months dragged on with no word, no money. He thought about the sacrifices he had made, and the debt that seemed to grow heavier with each passing week.

Many Black veterans, like Parson, chose to stay in the South after their discharge. They became leaders, holding communities together through the storms of Reconstruction. Meanwhile, white regiments were sent home quickly, their sacrifices celebrated, and their futures secured. The War Department claimed white soldiers "deserved" the first chance to return to civilian life, as if Black soldiers' years of service and suffering counted for less.

Spring turned to summer, and then to fall. The demobilization of the USCT regiments was a slow bleed. White officers and men left Texas, heading north for their final pay and discharge, while Black soldiers remained behind, tasked with enforcing the very policies that kept them from their families. Supplies were tight, tempers short, and the sense of injustice grew sharper each day.

One of Parson's comrades wrote to Edwin Stanton, the Secretary of War, pleading for understanding. He asked why the Black soldiers, already battered by years of war and separation, were being asked to give even more. Many fell ill, worn down by the harsh conditions and the constant ache of missing loved ones. Even the Confederate prisoners, once enemies, were sent home quickly to clear out the overcrowded camps.

Parson believed the government's refusal to demobilize the USCT regiments had real, human consequences. The wives and children of Black soldiers waited and suffered, their futures suspended by official indifference. The promise of reunion, of healing, was denied by bureaucratic inertia and old prejudice.

Finally, in February 1866, the 1st USCT Cavalry Regiment was mustered out. Parson had spent months on the Rio Grande and at other lonely posts in Texas, but now he could see the end. He often thought of Frances and the moment she would see him in uniform, the proof of all he had endured. He hoped she might stand with him, shoulder to shoulder, when the next challenge came.

Parson's story was not unique, but it was his own. In every step, every choice, he carried the weight of history — the pain of the past, the uncertainty of the future, and the stubborn hope that freedom, once begun, could not be unmade. In the air of Southampton, thick with cherry blossoms and memory, Parson set his sights not just on survival, but on the slow, stubborn work of creating a world where his children, and Frances's, could walk unafraid in the light.

While Parson was on leave, he learned that the Civil Rights Act of 1866 had been passed, overriding President Johnson's veto. A surge of elation washed over him, his chest swelling with pride and a smile stretching across his face. Like the Republican lawmakers in the United States Congress, Parson believed the Federal government had a role in shaping an integrated society in the seceded states. He opposed President

Johnson's plan for Reconstruction. He was happy that it was overruled, which would have led to a different approach.

At the Bureau, an agent informed him that Congress had passed several statutes aimed at protecting the rights of the formerly enslaved, many of which had been vetoed by President Andrew Johnson. One such law was the Civil Rights Act. It declared that all people born in the United States were U.S. citizens. It stated that all had certain inalienable rights, including the right to enter into contracts, own property, sue in court, and enjoy the complete protection of federal law.

The Act granted the U.S. district courts exclusive jurisdiction over criminal cases related to violations of the Act. In addition, it granted concurrent jurisdiction, along with the U.S. circuit courts, over all civil and criminal cases affecting individuals who could not enforce the rights guaranteed by the act in state court.

The act established that all persons born in the United States were citizens and entitled to the same fundamental rights, regardless of race or previous condition of servitude. This landmark legislation, passed after the Civil War, aimed to protect the civil rights of newly freed Black people and ensure their equal standing under the law.

During the subsequent legislative process, Congress deleted a key provision that prohibited discrimination in civil rights or immunities among the nation's inhabitants on account of race, color, or previous condition of servitude. On April 5, 1866, the Senate overrode President Johnson's veto. This marked the first time that the U.S. Congress ever overrode a presidential veto for a significant piece of legislation.

During their furlough, Parson and Solomon discussed the Freedmen's Bureau hearing. The hearing concerned the assault and battery case of Edward "Ned" Sykes, who was an assumed freed relative. According to the conversation, Ned Sykes and William M. Beaton, who owned a store and a cotton gin at Boykins Depot in Southampton, had a confrontation. Ned claimed that Beaton had assaulted him with a wooden door bar; Beaton did not deny the accusation but said that Ned had first pulled a knife on him.

Lieutenant Deacon gathered testimony about the incident, which occurred in December 1866, and held a hearing. All witnesses to the case agreed that the trouble developed in Beaton's store. The two men got into an argument after Ned requested pay for packing cotton at Beaton's gin. Beaton gave Ned thirty or forty cents worth of cheese, saying he would settle for whatever else he owed later.

Ned complained, whereupon Beaton ordered Sykes to leave the store. Ned replies by saying something to the effect that "the law was as much for one man as another." Ned's behavior enraged Beaton, who chased him out of the store and knocked Ned bloody and senseless with the door bar.

Beaton's principal witness was Thomas Archer, his store clerk. Archer testified that Ned, who was drunk, came into the store requesting cheese and crackers. Archer, under orders not to sell to Ned on credit, referred Ned to Beaton, who offered him cheese and crackers in payment for whatever work he had done that day. Ned maintained that Beaton should pay him in cash. Beaton, promising to settle fairly with Ned after he was sober, ordered Ned to leave the store.

Ned, however, refused to leave, and the standoff became tense. Beaton, angered, finally announced to him: "I have heard enough of this, and if you won't go out, I'll see if I can't make you." Archer reported that Ned thereupon retreated out of the store, while holding a knife in a "threatening attitude" and says in substance, "I am out now. I dare you or any other man to strike me."

At that point, Beaton attacked Ned with the door bar. When he recovered, he vowed to go to Jerusalem to lodge a complaint with Lieutenant Deacon and have justice served upon him. Beaton thereupon warned Ned that if he went to the Bureau officer, he should "take himself off his plantation and never come there anymore." Ned, nevertheless, went the next day to see Deacon.

The troubles between Ned and Beaton took place in December 1866. Seven months later, Lieutenant Deacon held a hearing on the case. The settlement, a compromise of sorts, vindicated Ned. He received $100 from Beaton to compensate for the "assault and battery" he had suffered. Ned promised to drop any further prosecution of the case. Deacon left no record of the basis for his decision. The settlement acknowledged that Beaton had wrongfully injured Ned.

In the last days of Parson's furlough and leading up to his return to duty, Louisa extended an invitation to family and friends to join them at their cabin. The gathering served as a celebration of Parson's return home following his self-liberation. Louisa decorated their cabin with themes symbolizing their newfound freedom, independence, and aspirations. After emancipation, formerly enslaved Black people often decorated their homes and settlements. Louisa created a welcoming environment, and her presence and support made a significant difference.

Louisa prepared Parson's favorite dishes or recreated a traditional meal they might have missed while away. During the celebration, attendees took a moment to acknowledge his bravery, resilience, and the sacrifices he made during his service. Guests exchanged anecdotes of their time while he was away to help him catch up on what he missed and the turbulent times since the war.

Everyone was happy and excited to celebrate Parson's return. They observed some changes and adjustments in him, but a feeling of joy and pride accompanied these upon seeing him. He was eager to reconnect with Frances and sought information about her from the guest. According to Parthenia, Jacob Williams' daughter, Frances, still lived on an adjacent farm and was known as Kindred, the name her family gave her when they owned her. As Parthenia looked around, she observed Frances entering the celebration.

She appeared elegantly dressed, in a fitted bodice, a full skirt, and a corset, which created a charming silhouette. The iconic hoop undergarment made her look like a picture featured in the Harper's Bazaar fashion magazine, but in a more subtle way. Using leftover fabric found abandoned, she created the outfit herself. Frances learned to sew from her mother and became a skillful seamstress. While enslaved, she earned extra money for her master by sewing for his friends and acquaintances.

Parson's time with family and Frances restored his energy, allowing him to appreciate his achievement before his furlough ended and the hard work started again. Parson had survived death, overcome his greatest fear, defeated the Army of Northern Virginia, and now earned the freedom that he sought. Parson gained honor, greater knowledge, and insight while fighting in the Civil War. He had earned the right to celebrate freedom, citizenship, and equality.

During the celebration, Parson discussed his connection to Sargent Etheridge and Chaplain Turner, who provided information on resources available to USCT veterans, as well as financial and homestead benefits. He elaborated on how these men, through their dedicated service, provided crucial information regarding healthcare options tailored for veterans. He described educational programs designed to aid their transition back into civilian life, as well as valuable training opportunities to enhance their skills and employability. He credited them for his knowledge and insight, a newfound wisdom, and a deeper understanding of himself.

Solomon summoned Parson to address the guests, who were eagerly gathered to honor him. He paused, reflecting on the newly planted cherry tree and comparing it to his self-liberation. Next, Parson stated that freedom, citizenship, and equality are like cherry blossoms, and whether they bear fruit depends on how well they are cared for. Parson said, "If a cherry tree produces blossoms but no fruit, then the potential causes of this non-bearing should be investigated."

Cherry trees will fruit when they become old enough and are allowed to blossom freely. Most cherry tree problems result from cultural practices, climate, and weather of the cherry tree or orchard. Like cherry trees, most human and civil rights issues come from the country's social, economic, and political problems. Self-liberation capability, a crucial aspect of formal education, land acquisition, and voting, are essential for freedom, citizenship, and equality. The four million newly freed people held the reins for shaping fruitful movements of unbiased emancipation.

Having returned to Southampton County, Parson was transformed, bringing with him a greater knowledge of and insight into freedom, which he eagerly shared with his family and settlement. Even though he left the farm as a fugitive from enslavement, Parson returned home as a highly skilled advocate for human and civil rights, educating his children and becoming a landowner. After celebrating with family, friends, and settlement members, he returned to Fort Monroe early the next morning to complete his enlistment.

Upon his return to Fort Monroe after his furlough, Parson discovered that the Johnson administration had not delivered on its promise of providing forty acres of abandoned and confiscated land. Upon hearing the disappointing news, a surge of anger coursed through Parson's veins, causing his heart rate to increase and his muscles to tense up. The disappointment of an unfulfilled promise felt like a physical burden on his shoulders.

The combination of military and legislative efforts led formerly enslaved people to believe compensation was achievable. Congress established the Freedmen's Bureau to help them transition from enslavement to freedom. The Act empowered the Bureau to lease confiscated or abandoned land, up to forty acres, to freedpeople and loyal white refugees for three-year terms.

However, President Johnson's Amnesty Proclamation of May 29, 1865, reversed these efforts. Circular No. 15, issued by the Bureau on September 12, 1865, coupled with Johnson's presidential pardons, provided for the restoration of land to former owners. Because of President Johnson's restoration program, freedpeople, except for a small number who held legal land titles, were removed from the land.

This led to the reversal of Sherman's order and the eviction of thousands of freed people from the land they had cultivated. Except for those who had legal titles, the land was restored to its former owners. This reversal left many freed people without land. It forced them into exploitative systems like sharecropping, which often perpetuated cycles of poverty and debt. This undermined the potential for economic independence that landownership promised.

Although Congress later debated measures like the "Second Freedmen's Bureau bill," which sought to extend the Bureau's powers and resources, and the Southern Homestead Act, intended to make public lands in the South available to Black families. These initiatives faced vehement opposition from President Andrew Johnson, who favored a more lenient approach towards the former Confederate states. Johnson's resistance manifested in numerous vetoes, effectively blocking the expansion of the Bureau and hindering its ability to protect the rights of Black Americans.

Moreover, even when laws like the Southern Homestead Act were passed, they proved ineffective in significantly redistributing land to formerly enslaved people. Other factors affecting the situation included poor land quality, limited access to credit and resources, and continued resistance from white landowners. The failure to provide formerly enslaved people with land ownership, a crucial element of economic independence, undermined the promise of Reconstruction and contributed to the perpetuation of racial inequality in the South.

Parson continued communicating with formerly enslaved neighbors in Cross Keys about the challenging and oppressive situation that had happened while he was away. He began to reestablish his life with his family and a new home. Before being discharged and returning to Southampton County, Parson expanded his knowledge of land ownership and the ongoing struggle among freed people to acquire abandoned and confiscated land.

Having been discharged at Fort Monroe in December 1867, Parson and his brothers, Joseph and Henry, concluded their military service and subsequently embarked on a tour of the Hampton Institute. Despite ongoing discrimination, they had secured a lasting position within the military by the time their service concluded. The emotional journey they went through had a profound impact on them physically and was reflected in their physical strength. They emerged from the Army stronger than before, with a newfound sense of confidence and inner strength radiating through their posture and demeanor.

Upon his discharge from Fort Monroe, Parson suggested they go on a tour of the Hampton Normal and Agricultural Institute, a historically Black college dedicated to the education of formerly enslaved people and their descendants. Suggesting the tour to his brothers, he said, "A normal school, college, or normal institute trains teachers in the norms of pedagogy and curriculum." The visit provided Parson with insights into the possibilities of education and self-improvement for Black settlements in the post-Civil War South.

Parson first heard about the school for Black children started by Mary Peake when he enlisted in the Army in 1864. She instructed the students in reading, writing, arithmetic, geography, grammar, and various household skills. Her classes, initially held under an oak tree, were for children and adults seeking education during the Civil War. This school, supported by the AMA, is considered a precursor to Hampton University, which was officially founded in 1868.

In 1866, under the leadership of Brigadier General Samuel Chapman Armstrong, the institute initially focused on providing practical skills and teacher training to empower newly emancipated Black Americans. Its curriculum combined academic studies with vocational training in areas such as agriculture, carpentry, and domestic science, reflecting the belief that economic self-sufficiency was crucial for the progress of Black people.

With his enlightening experience at Hampton Normal and Agricultural Institute, Parson prepared to return to Southampton County, to reunite with family or to contribute to the rebuilding efforts in his home settlement. After the tour, he visited the sutlers to purchase a ready-to-wear clothing outfit, similar to those worn by the formerly enslaved people he observed on and around Hampton's campus. Sutlers offered a variety of manufactured clothing, including shirts, pants, and hats, as well as goods for soldiers who wanted to have or make civilian garments for themselves.

The institute officially became Hampton University in 1984. The name change reflected the school's expanded academic offerings and overall advancement. Hampton University boasts a long and impressive list of distinguished alumni across various fields. Among them are Booker T. Washington, the founder of Tuskegee Institute, and Robert Sengstacke Abbott, founder of the Chicago Defender. Other prominent figures include actor and comedian Wanda Sykes, NASA mathematician and engineer Mary Jackson, and Alberta Williams King, the mother of Martin Luther King Jr.

Parson witnessed the Congress as it continued to pass increasingly radical legislation. After his discharge, he experienced a significant decrease in his personal hatred, depression, and other character flaws, due to the insights he had gained during the war. The Act outlines the legal rights granted to all citizens, ensuring equality and fairness under the law. Specifically, it grants all citizens the same legal rights, including the right to enter into contracts, allowing them to agree to terms and be bound by them. However, despite the promises of the act, Parson saw that anti-Black violence aimed to restore white domination in Southampton County.

The Civil Rights Act established the right to own property, enabling citizens to acquire, possess, and dispose of assets as they see fit. Parson experienced feelings of empowerment and freedom that could manifest physically in various ways. It led to a decrease in stress levels, improved his overall well-being, and a boost in energy and motivation to make the most out of their assets. In addition, it gave him a sense of lightness and freedom as he felt unburdened by oppressive constraints, allowing him to fully enjoy the benefits of his emancipation.

The Civil Rights Act had also guaranteed Parson the right to sue in court, providing a mechanism for citizens to seek redress for grievances and enforce their legal rights. In the hushed solemnity of the Freedmen's Bureau courtroom, he had witnessed the rustle of papers as lawyers prepared their arguments. He had breathed in the air, thick with anticipation, and smelled faintly of old pine wood and floor wax. Watching the exercise of the civil and criminal law had felt palpable, a heavy cloak of justice draped over the proceedings. The newly freed Black plaintiff's heart would pound with a mix of hope and trepidation. He finally found a voice against injustice.

This Act empowered the federal courts to enforce and protect these newly defined civil rights, giving them explicit jurisdiction over cases involving violations of the Act. This meant that individuals who believed their rights had been violated under the act could now bring their cases directly to federal court, bypassing state courts that might be less sympathetic or effective in upholding these federal protections. The increased role of the federal courts marked a significant shift in the balance of power, enabling more consistent and robust enforcement of civil rights nationwide.

Thanks to the Civil Rights Act, Parson secured citizenship and received equal legal protection. It epitomized a federal plan for human and civil rights aimed at integrating Black Americans into society. It defined American citizenship and outlined the rights that come with it. It also made it illegal to deny anyone citizenship rights based on race, color, or past enslavement or involuntary servitude.

The primary objective of the Act was to safeguard the civil rights of newly emancipated Black people. It aimed to ensure their equal standing under the law. It also gave U.S. district courts exclusive jurisdiction over criminal cases that violated the Act. Additionally, it provided concurrent jurisdiction with federal circuit courts over all civil and criminal cases. This was for individuals who could not enforce their rights in state courts.

Racism and discrimination caused ongoing oppression for Black people in Virginia. However, Parson's service in the USCT earned him trust and respect within the Black settlement. His journey to self-discovery shaped his character, making self-renewal a habit. He started planning activities and scheduling them to create a routine. This routine led to what he called an upward spiral of self-liberation, making freedom feel natural.

CHAPTER SEVEN

The Fourteenth Amendment Ratified

On May 29, 1866, the House of Representatives introduced a joint resolution proposing the Fourteenth Amendment to the U.S. Constitution. A pivotal piece of legislation in the aftermath of the Civil War, it addressed citizenship, equal protection, and other fundamental rights. It contains several notable rights and protections, such as citizenship for Black people, applying due process, and granting equal protection under State laws.

Parson joyously opined that the Amendment was the most remarkable achievement and accomplishment of the Congressional Reconstruction. A wide, unrestrained smile stretched across his face while he spoke. As he explained with enthusiasm, the benefits of the constitutional Amendment included the prevention of discrimination or any other violations of a citizen's rights and protections by state agents or government entities. It prohibited racial discrimination in public accommodations and was unconstitutional because it tried to regulate private actors.

As he read the proposed Amendment, a wave of relief washed over him, easing the struggle against discrimination and other rights violations from his shoulders. His heart raced with a mix of excitement for the future and apprehension for what lay ahead. The physical effects of these emotions were palpable as he contemplated the next chapter of his life.

As proposed, the Amendment affirmed that the apportionment of representatives in the Federal government would be based on the population of each state. The abolition of enslavement meant that the representation of formerly enslaved people in the House of Representatives increased. The Fourteenth Amendment included a clause designed to pressure former Confederate states into enfranchising Black citizens.

It disqualified an individual from serving as a state or federal official if that person had "engaged in insurrection or rebellion against" the United States. Although written during the Civil War, theoretically, it still applied to the disqualification of members of future rebellions or insurrections against the United States.

The proposed Amendment declared the national debt valid and rejected the Confederate debt. Despite this, a federal court ruled in 1883 that it would not honor contracts related to Confederate debt. Nonetheless, it enforced contracts using Confederate money to protect individuals who were compelled to accept it during the Civil War. The fourth section contained a constitutional clause that ensured the government would pay its debts, particularly those incurred during wars. This also prevented the government from taking on or covering the debts of those who revolted against it.

Finally, it empowered Congress to enact legislation enforcing the rights and protections of the Amendment. As Parson explained, this allowed Congress to counteract state actions infringing upon these rights, effectively enabling the correction of conflicting state laws. Without this provision, Congress lacked the authority to enforce the Amendment's limits on government power.

As his furlough ended, Parson negotiated a Freedmen's Bureau-approved labor contract with Jacob Williams before leaving Southampton County. This contract outlined the terms of Parson's employment, specifying wages, hours, and responsibilities. It should protect him from exploitation while providing Williams with a dependable workforce. The government's involvement suggests an attempt to ensure fair treatment and prevent the re-establishment of exploitative practices reminiscent of enslavement.

The Bureau's system of contracts between landlords and laborers was the most promising solution to this dilemma. Contracts outlined the rights and obligations of both parties, ensuring landlords of a reliable, competent workforce while simultaneously guaranteeing that free laborers receive fair wages and treatment. The Bureau agents arranged it based on a wage rate comparable to that for hiring a non-disabled man, with the pay going to the master. Subsequently, Parson accepted the bureau-approved labor contract with Jacob Williams.

On December 4, 1867, after serving three years, the Union Army discharged Parson from military service at Fort Monroe. Virginia was still under martial law, pending the adoption of a constitution that would guarantee civil liberties for formerly enslaved people. Throughout his growth journey, Parson faced and overcame numerous failures, crises, and bouts of self-doubt.

Although recognition and acceptance never came easily for Black soldiers in the Army, by the end of the Civil War, Parson boasted that they had secured a permanent role in the federal military establishment. This federal presence, particularly in Southampton, proved beneficial, as numerous Black veterans found careers in politics during the Congressional Reconstruction. They served as delegates to Virginia's state constitutional conventions, won elections to state legislatures, and even to Congress.

After returning to Southampton County, Virginia, Parson, a recently freed enslaved person seeking economic opportunity, accepted a Freedmen's Bureau-approved labor contract with Jacob Williams, a local landowner. Parson learned that Solomon Sykes accepted a written work contract with Jacob Williams. The Bureau faced a terrifying task in reconciling the claims of the former enslavers and the enslaved people.

Parson Sykes persevered through numerous failures, crises, and bouts of self-doubt throughout his labor contract. This period coincided with Congress's significantly expanded role in Reconstruction in 1867, as it overrode President Johnson's vetoes to pass landmark legislation. In particular, the

Civil Rights Act, which granted birthright citizenship, the Reconstruction Act of 1867, which outlined the terms for readmitting the Confederate states, and the ratification of the Fourteenth Amendment.

At family gatherings, Parson recounted how he and other Black veterans faced a career filled with both promise and prejudice. Usually sitting around his favored cherry tree, he described the racism and discrimination that led to ongoing oppression for Black soldiers. However, many of them found that their military service had earned them trust and respect, at least within the Black settlements. They survived death, overcame pay inequality, defeated the Army of Northern Virginia, weathered systematic efforts to deny them fundamental civil rights, and now earned the freedom, citizenship, and equality they sought.

Parson discovered the proposed Fourteenth Amendment. This Amendment granted citizenship and federal civil rights to all individuals, including formerly enslaved people. As Parson recalled, on June 16, 1866, Congress submitted the Joint Resolution proposing the Amendment to the states for ratification. On July 28, 1868, the Secretary of State announced that the Amendment, having been ratified by twenty-eight of the thirty-seven states, was now part of the supreme law of the land. The proposed constitutional Amendment guaranteed U.S. citizenship. Furthermore, it granted federal civil rights to all individuals, including Solomon, Louisa, and Frances.

Parson felt the Amendment made him equal under the law. He believed he deserved equal protection against any discrimination and any incitement to such discrimination. He understood that the Amendment ensured that anyone born or naturalized within the United States was a citizen. Further, no state could deny any person within its jurisdiction the equal protection of the laws.

During Reconstruction, the Federal government aimed to integrate formerly enslaved people into society by granting them citizenship and voting rights. While the Amendment granted Black people the rights of citizenship, this did not immediately translate into the ability to vote. Officials at many state polling places systematically rejected Black voters. Decades later, a major goal of the twentieth-century civil rights movement remained securing and protecting full voting rights for all Black people.

Parson learned that the enfranchisement of Southampton's formerly enslaved people refers to the process of granting legal rights and freedoms. He described it as the process by which the nation fulfilled its promise to grant the right to vote to formerly enslaved people. This occurred through the passage of the Fourteenth Amendment. A significant provision of the Amendment was to grant citizenship to all persons born or naturalized in the United States. Thereby, it granted citizenship to formerly enslaved people.

Another equally important provision was the statement that "nor shall any state deprive any person of life, liberty, or property, without due process of law; nor deny to any person within its jurisdiction the equal protection of the laws." The right to due process of law and equal protection under the law now applies to both the federal and state governments.

One significant legacy of Reconstruction was the resolute effort by both Black and White citizens to realize the promise of equality preserved in the Constitution. Besides not extending the Bill of Rights to states, the Amendment also proved ineffective in protecting the rights of Black people. They turned to petitions and lawsuits, Congress passed laws, and the executive branch attempted to enforce measures to safeguard their rights. Even though Black people could not fully realize the potential of the Amendment during Reconstruction, they presented persuasive arguments and dissenting opinions. Parson held that these ideas led to substantial changes in the 20th century.

As Parson's passion for agribusiness and politics grew, he became increasingly engaged in state and local politics. Following the suspension of regular warfare, Parson revealed that the ensuing struggle was a bitter one, racially polarized, and interwoven with political and economic factors. Specifically, the formerly enslaved people in Southampton County, who had been previously subordinated, were energized by newfound opportunities. The presence of federal troops provided some protection for Black citizens. Still, their numbers often did not prevent widespread disenfranchisement and the undermining of Reconstruction policies by local authorities sympathetic to the former Confederate states.

In the spring of 1865, the County found itself under military rule and occupation. The formerly enslaved people and their allies clashed with white landowners and former Confederates over issues of land ownership, labor contracts, voting rights, and access to education. Local chapters of the Union League organized Black voters. They advocated for Republican candidates, while white conservatives formed groups like the Ku Klux Klan to intimidate Black residents and suppress their political participation through violence and economic coercion.

Military occupation provided a crucial presence to protect Black citizens from violence and intimidation by white supremacist groups and former Confederates. Military authorities exercised formidable power between 1867 and 1869, enrolling Black voters and ensuring fair elections. They appointed civilian officials for both state and local government. This temporary situation challenged the unquestioned dominance that white people in Southampton had always enjoyed.

After the authorization of the Bureau, he learned that General Howard's July 12, 1865, directive authorized the appointment of a Bureau official in each state to superintend the development of schools. Parson noted that the Freedmen's Bureau also did what it could to promote schooling and educational opportunities. Howard allowed them the choice of working alongside state officials or with the charitable groups supporting his field operations. The Bureau would not establish schools on its own. Instead, it took awareness of all that was being done to educate refugees and formerly enslaved people, secure proper protection for schools and teachers, and promote method and efficiency.

The principal function of the Bureau was to make the Freedmen a self-supporting class of free laborers who would understand the necessity of steady employment and the responsibility of providing for themselves and their families. If laborers refuse employment offered on terms ensuring comfortable subsistence and freedom from idleness and dependence on charity, treat them as vagrants. Parson read Bureau letters and reports, penned by both Southampton residents and federal officials who lived in or oversaw county affairs during the Reconstruction years.

Freed Black people who required no other support from a landlord might contract to receive between one-third and one-half of specified crops such as corn, cotton, peas, and potatoes; some landlords reduced the brandy share to one-sixth. More typical were crop shares of between one-quarter and one-third, with landowners obligated to provide food, clothing, and quarters. He observed a variety of arrangements used with the freed people.

Parson recalled the investigations into violence, threats, and intimidation that had plagued the Black settlements in Southampton County. By mid-1867, astonished whites discovered that Black people in large numbers had registered to vote, and that may have triggered increased violence and intimidation. The formerly enslaved people in 1867 may also have become emboldened to sue in their courts. Pogroms against

Black people, including large-scale massacres like the one that occurred in Memphis in 1866, were an unfortunate reality of Reconstruction. He specifically remembered the case involving the anonymous threatening notes sent to Black agribusiness owners and the subsequent vandalism incidents targeting their properties.

Southampton whites used various forms of intimidation, including verbal threats, property destruction, and threatening letters, to discourage Black citizens from exercising their newly acquired rights. Faced with violence, intimidation, and discrimination, formerly enslaved people and women fought back in small and large ways, reporting outrages to Freedmen's Bureau agents, testifying in court, seeking just compensation, protecting fellow settlement members, and more.

Lieutenant Deacon resolved several cases in Southampton County. The Bureau documented numerous cases of beatings, whippings, and other physical assaults against formerly enslaved people. In one report, Deacon worked out a compromise settlement between Randolph Stokes, a formerly enslaved person, and James S. Harrison, whom Stokes accused of assault and battery. Deacon fined Joseph Barham $40 for assaulting Ephriam Ford, a formerly enslaved person, intending to kill.

In another case, the limited jurisdiction of the court established for formerly enslaved people appears to have restricted Deacon. When James and Albert Artis charged Chestine Magget with discharging the contents of a double-barreled shotgun at them, Deacon referred the case to the circuit court. Deacon required the civil authorities to impose a $400 bond on Magget to ensure his appearance.

Lieutenant Deacon conducted investigations into two incidents in which formerly enslaved people were the apparent victims of violent abuse. Because he transcribed testimony from witnesses in both cases, Deacon's reports provide significant firsthand evidence about Southampton society during the first turbulent years after the enslavement system ended. The agent also settled the case in which Nelson Davis, a formerly enslaved person, complained that he was driven away without cause by Abner Stephenson. Davis won the right to return to his home and job, and Stephenson agreed "to have nothing more to do with Davis."

Bureau agents, according to Parson, helped settle legal issues, ensured labor contracts were fair, and occasionally asked federal authorities to intervene when local officials could not or would not protect freed people.

Parson remembered the unsuccessful inquiry into Caroline Drewry's death, from violent abuse. Putnam sent Lieutenant Deacon to investigate the murder, attempted murder, beatings, whippings, or other physical assaults against Caroline, a freedwoman in Southampton County. On June 27, 1867, Caroline died under mysterious circumstances, the apparent victim of violent abuse. Deacon conducted investigations into the incident involving her death.

Her son, George Drewry, reported that his mother's injuries included bruises on her hands and head, plus kicking.

Pains in her head, neck, side, and breast prevented her from sleeping that night. Despite being able to do laundry and prepare dinner for the following morning, Caroline Drewry passed away in the early afternoon, a day after her assault. At the behest of Joseph W. Claud, a prominent local justice of the peace, the court assembled twelve white jurors to examine Caroline Drewry's body and investigate her death the next day.

Lieutenant Deacon's report provided firsthand evidence about racial violence in Southampton during the chaotic years after the enslavement of Black people ended. Given the instructions of Claud, the court selected twelve white jurors who concluded unanimously that Caroline came to her death from some unknown reason and not from any violence. Their conclusion relied on the testimony of two doctors who reported finding no evidence of violence while conducting a postmortem examination.

The official finding did not satisfy many formerly enslaved people in Southampton County, who suspected that Caroline Drewry died after being beaten by Dr. L. W. Jones. George Drewry quoted Jones as admitting that he had given Caroline Drewry "a good flailing" because she had her two elder sons, George Drewry and Henry Ivey, away. They testified that on the day before Caroline died, their younger brother and sister came running to say that Dr. Jones was beating their mother. The older brothers, who had been visiting Henry Ivey's father on a neighboring farm, ran back to confront Jones, who, they insisted, had just stopped beating their mother with a stick.

The twelve white jurors concluded unanimously that "the deceased came to her death from some unknown cause and not from any violence." Their conclusion relied on the testimony of two doctors who reported finding no evidence of violence while conducting a postmortem examination.

The legal sequel to Caroline Drewry's death was predictable. Deacon arrested Jones and required him to post a $1,000 bond as a promise of his appearance. Deacon's superiors in Richmond refused, however, to reopen the case against Jones, believing that any prosecution for murder would be useless. Acknowledging the testimony of her sons, a judge advocate ruled that the report by the two physicians would prevent any conviction, even though they had failed to make a proper postmortem examination.

Lieutenant Deacon faced significant challenges in his efforts to combat racial violence. The Bureau lacked adequate resources to address the scale of violence and intimidation because of underfunding and understaffing. Despite its limitations, the government's documentation of violence provides valuable insight into the struggles witnessed by Parson during Reconstruction and the continued resistance to racial equality in the former Confederate states.

Frustrated by the inability to secure complete emancipation in Southampton, Parson and his neighbors within his settlement then sought the right to vote. Faced with these oppressive conditions, the ballot offered a ray of hope. Black people understood that gaining the right to vote was crucial for influencing political decisions, securing their rights, and improving their lives.

Black people in Southampton embraced this opportunity with fervor, organizing and participating in elections, even at significant personal risk. Their participation in the political process during Reconstruction led to the election of Black representatives to state and federal offices, demonstrating their determination to forge a new future despite the numerous obstacles they faced.

Congress empowered military authority to oversee and supersede civil authority in the ten recalcitrant former rebel states. As a first step in organizing new governments, Congress ordered elections in each state to choose delegates for constitutional conventions. To ensure that Unionists gained the upper hand over ex-rebels, Congress specified that all adult males of both races could vote except for those who failed to pass specific tests of loyalty.

The formerly enslaved people could vote, but many white men could not. Moreover, federal officials took charge of registering voters and administering the elections for delegates to the constitutional convention. Directives from military authorities in Richmond spelled out in close detail how the registration process should proceed and who was eligible to vote. Lieutenant Deacon, appointed president of the county Board of Registration on April 15, could choose three registers at-large and one registering officer for each magisterial district, of which there were seven in Southampton.

He was to choose "deserving, loyal citizens" who had "the confidence of all classes" and could take the "ironclad oath," affirming they had never voluntarily aided the Confederacy. The three registers-at-large would receive compensation at the quite handsome rate of $125 per month; the district officials were to receive $5 per day, including reasonable travel allowances.

The military authorities in Richmond issued specific guidelines regarding eligibility. All male citizens aged twenty-one or older and who had lived in Virginia for one year, "of whatever race, color, or previous condition," were eligible to take the oath and register. The guidelines allowed eligibility, "except such as may be disfranchised for participation in the rebellion, or felony."

Deacon soon selected three registrars-at-large and six district registrars. None of the registrars-at-large had voted in Southampton in 1860-61, but all six of the district registrars were Union Whigs. Deacon organized his nine appointees into three teams, each comprising three members. Their jurisdiction included the Drewrysville district in the southwestern corner of the County, as well as the Franklin district, wedged between the Nottoway and Blackwater rivers.

Black men, most of whom were former slaves, were loyal and therefore eligible to register, provided they had lived in the state for at least a year. Eagerly seizing the opportunity to affirm their new rights, they registered in large numbers. White men, dismayed that Black people could register, could not assume their eligibility. Even if white eligibility standards were less strict than the written rules, officials could challenge ineligible registrants using established procedures.

In Southampton and across the former Confederate states, cherry blossoms became a symbol of hope for many Black people. Despite the destruction and devastation brought upon the country, the cherry blossoms continued to bloom each spring, offering a sense of resilience, renewal, and optimism for the future. Like the blooming trees in groomed orchards, they stand as a powerful symbol of citizenship, equality, and justice in defining humanity.

On October 8, 1869, more than a year after its ratification and adoption into the U.S. Constitution, Virginia officially ratified the Fourteenth Amendment. The enfranchisement of Southampton's formerly enslaved people stands out as the most startling single development in the County's political history. As it took place, Union Whigs attempted to create a biracial Union Republican party, with white leadership and a primarily Black electorate.

When Black people rejected that overture, white Whigs joined with white Democrats to create the local Conservative party, and Southampton politics became racially polarized. Few native white Virginians were more thoroughly out of sympathy with the Confederacy or more eager to see the state reconstructed than Dr. Thomas Jefferson Pretlow, the heir of Southampton's most prominent Quaker family.

During the summer of 1867, the white Southampton Unionists supporting John Pretlow's candidacy considered themselves Republicans. On July 27, they held a meeting at Franklin. They nominated seven delegates to the state Republican convention in Richmond in early August. A new constitution, which provided universal adult suffrage, was finally passed by voters on July 6, 1869. On October 8, 1869, Virginia voted to ratify the constitutional Amendment as part of the requirement for being readmitted to the Union.

On January 26, 1870, President Ulysses S. Grant signed the act that readmitted Virginia to the Union. This act also permitted the state to form its own militias. This marked the end of shaping the policies and processes for reintegration in Virginia. Virginia rejoined the Union in January 1870, marking the beginning of the next segment of Reconstruction, which lasted from the moment civil authorities resumed power until the Army finally withdrew from its Southern occupation in 1877.

In 1868, Congress enacted legislation allowing former Confederate states, once they had reentered the Union, to create militias. Following its January 1870 return to the Union, Virginia reinstated the Virginia Volunteers in 1871. Reconstruction governments implemented an all-volunteer militia system in Virginia, diverging from the previous compulsory service model. Richmond saw the formation of the Attucks Guard, the state's first official Black militia unit, named after the first person killed in the Boston Massacre. Other Black militia units followed.

The same law also established the basic outline of the militia. In Virginia, each volunteer company comprised between 50 and 100 men, with six to ten of these companies forming a regiment. Enlistees, who served for five years, supplied their uniforms while the state provided arms and equipment. The men elected their officers, who appointed noncommissioned officers. Robert L. Hobson, a barber, was appointed the first captain of the Attucks Guard.

The readmission to the Union, coupled with the re-establishment of the militia system in a modified form, signified a crucial stage in Virginia's post-Civil War history. This period mirrored the profound societal and political transformations characteristic of the Reconstruction era. These units did see active service in 1887, when they were activated to quell a violent longshoremen's strike.

During Reconstruction, the Federal government aided formerly enslaved Black Americans in their transition to freedom. John Mercer Langston, a prominent abolitionist, attorney, educator, and politician, joined the Freedmen's Bureau as an agent observing schools in Virginia. On June 17, 1867, the Bureau appointed him general inspector of schools. In his role, he advocated for educational opportunities and legal rights for formerly enslaved people.

His commitment to education led to his involvement in the establishment of Virginia State University in 1882, the first fully state-supported four-year institution of higher learning for Black students in Virginia. Langston's work with the Freedmen's Bureau and his role in founding Virginia State University highlight his dedication to empowering Black Americans through education and ensuring their full participation in American society.

Langston grew up in Ohio and graduated from Oberlin College in 1849. He earned his MA in 1852 and graduated from the college's seminary in 1853. Also, Langston studied law and was admitted to the bar in 1854. In 1855, Langston won election as clerk of the township of Brownhelm, making him one of the first Black Americans to hold elective office in Ohio. He quickly became a significant figure in the abolitionist movement and in the state's nascent Republican Party.

In 1870, Langston became dean of Howard University's law school and served as acting president of the university from 1873 until 1875. He continued to be an active member of the Republican Party. In 1871, President Ulysses S. Grant appointed him to the Board of Health for the District of Columbia. Howard awarded an honorary LLD to Langston in 1874. In 1877, President Rutherford B. Hayes appointed him Minister Resident and Consul General to Haiti, a post he served in until resigning in 1885.

On November 19, 1885, the Virginia State Board of Education appointed Langston president of the newly established Virginia Normal and Collegiate Institute, located on the campus near Petersburg. He was accepted in December and took office in January 1886. One of the principal purposes of the institute, the first state-supported college of its kind in the South, was to prepare Black American teachers for the state's public school system. It was pioneering in the South as well, being coeducational and employing both male and female instructors. The new school grew under his leadership, but the Democrat-packed board of visitors did not renew his contract two years later.

In 1888, he sought the Republican nomination for the U.S. House of Representatives. Langston ran an independent campaign in which a Democrat was named the winner. Langston disputed the election results; however, on September 23, 1890, after successfully contesting the election, Congress eventually seated him for the rest of his term.

The first Black American to win a seat in Congress from Virginia, Langston served only from September 23, 1890, to March 3, 1891. During the session, he sat on the Committee on Education.

Eventually, the Virginia Normal and Collegiate Institute became the first fully state-supported, four-year institution for Black Americans. In 1902, the legislature revised the charter act to curtail the collegiate program. It changed the name to Virginia Normal and Industrial Institute. In 1923, the program was restored, and in 1930, the name was changed to Virginia State College for Negroes.

The Norfolk division, added to the college in 1944, became a four-year branch in 1956. It gained independence as Norfolk State University in 1969. In 1979, the Virginia General Assembly changed its status and name to provide the present name, Virginia State University. Many of Parson's descendants have and continue to attend the two universities.

Parson geared up for the decisive fight, confronting the unexpected fallout from the Fourteenth Amendment, which was adopted into the U.S. Constitution. He knew that, after being adopted, these new rights and protections, despite their pledge of fairness, might have unpredictable and perilous results. He knew that the fight for true equality had just begun, and that vigilance and perseverance would be crucial in navigating the complexities and dangers of their newly acquired citizenship.

Parson knew that emancipation was only the first step, and that true freedom required education, economic stability, and a strong moral compass—all of which he aimed to provide to his flock, brick by painstaking brick. He sharpened his arguments, steeled his resolve, and prayed for the strength to guide his people through the turbulent waters ahead, knowing that the future of their settlement, and the nation, rested on his shoulders.

Parson now realized that Jacob feared his transformation and the hard-won freedom, citizenship, and equality that he could now enjoy, and a part of the reward was the fear of losing it. It heralded the end of Parson's character flaws and other inner conflicts that led to his turmoil. Furthermore, it encompasses several essential concepts, most notably state action, privileges, and immunities, citizenship, due process, and equal protection.

Parson's shift from fostering manipulation tactics to openly autonomy and self-determination exemplified the experiences of many other Black veterans. He came to understand that simply donning a uniform or signing up did not automatically grant him freedom.

For Parson, the constitutional Amendment provided the impetus to embrace the challenges of self-employment. It was also the inspiration behind the satisfying weight of land deeds held in his hand, as well as his commitment to helping family and neighbors pursue political offices.

The enfranchisement of Black citizens was the nation's most remarkable achievement of Reconstruction. Parson returned to Southampton County's familiar landscape and unfamiliar soundscape, where freedom rang out from cotton fields, voting boxes, and classrooms. He married Frances Hill in 1869; the rustle of her wedding dress was a whispered memory amidst the County's silent charm. He toiled in the sun-drenched fields he acquired as a farmer of gainful work, a reward to his soul after his discharge in December 1867.

With citizenship and civil rights secured, Parson was guaranteed freedom, liberty, and emancipation. His self-liberation journey's profound impact received constitutional recognition and commemoration. For Parson, the Amendment of the U.S. Constitution acknowledged and rewarded his heroism, bravery, meritorious service, and participation in the war. It granted citizenship to all people born or naturalized in the United States, including those formerly enslaved.

Parson joyfully claimed that the Amendment marked a significant step in enfranchising formerly enslaved people. In conjunction with the establishment of the Freedmen's Bureau to provide them with assistance in education, legal aid, and land acquisition, it extended human and civil rights to formerly enslaved people, which they had fought for and won.

CHAPTER EIGHT

The Fifteenth Amendment Ratified

Parson's story, like that of so many in Southampton County, is not just about a man freed from bondage. It is about a family torn apart and then, slowly—sometimes painfully—stitched back together in the aftermath of a war that promised freedom but delivered it unevenly. Parson's life is a window into what freedom meant on the ground: hope, struggle, heartbreak, and, sometimes, hard-won joy. The stakes for Parson were never philosophical. They were as real as the soil under his feet, as urgent as the hunger in his belly, as sharp as the memory of the whip's crack. When the Fifteenth Amendment was ratified in 1870, it promised to pull men like Parson and his kin from the shadows, to grant them a voice in a nation that had denied their humanity for generations. But as Parson learned, a promise on paper does not always make it so in the fields, the courthouses, or the streets.

Freedom for Parson began as a rumor, a whispered hope carried along the hedgerows and through the cabins. The war ended, but the world did not change overnight. For Parson and his brothers, the first taste of freedom was more survival than celebration. They clung to each other, building their lives from the ground up, even as they watched the old order claw its way back in new forms. The Thirteenth Amendment may have broken their chains, and the Fourteenth may have granted citizenship on paper, but it was the Fifteenth that promised them the power to shape their destinies—to vote, to be counted, to stand up and say, "I am here." The first time Parson registered to vote, standing shoulder to shoulder with other Black men, he felt the weight and the possibility of citizenship settle on his shoulders. It was a moment that reached beyond his own life, touching his parents' silent prayers and his children's future.

But history does not move in straight lines. Just as Parson allowed himself to imagine what might be possible, old fears and resentments flared anew. In Southampton, the same fields where he once toiled under the overseer's eye became battlegrounds for a new struggle. The memory of the Nat Turner Insurrection still haunted the county, fueling white anxieties and justifying new forms of control. Parson watched as Black men lined up to vote, only to be met by white men in hoods or uniforms, their faces hidden but their intentions unmistakable. The Black Codes, the rise of the Klan—these were not just distant headlines, but daily threats to his family, his neighbors, the fragile order they were trying to build.

For Parson, the fight to vote was inseparable from the fight to keep his family whole. The law had once denied even the right to marry. Now, with the end of slavery and the efforts of the Freedmen's Bureau, marriages like his to Frances— solemnized in the office of Doctor N. P. Barham, recorded and recognized—became acts of love and declarations of personhood. In marriage, Parson claimed what had been denied for generations: the right to form a family, to protect it, to pass on something more than sorrow. Together, he and Frances raised fourteen children, each one a living argument against a world that had tried to erase them.

Their union was not just personal, but political. To marry, to raise children, to own land and teach them to read— these were revolutionary acts in a society determined to keep Black people on the margins. Parson had seen what happened to families under slavery: the forced separations, the threats, the constant uncertainty. Now, every day that Frances and the children woke beneath the same roof, every meal they shared, every lesson he passed on, was a small victory, a piece of freedom made real. He held close the knowledge that the rights won in war and politics only mattered if they rooted themselves in daily life, in the bonds of family.

But the machinery of white supremacy was relentless. The language of the Fifteenth Amendment barred states from denying the right to vote based on race, color, or previous condition of servitude, but it left open the door to "race-neutral" obstacles: poll taxes, literacy tests, grandfather clauses, and outright intimidation. Parson saw firsthand how these new barriers sprang up, how the promise of equality was delayed, rerouted, sometimes snatched away entirely. The threats were not just legal; they were physical, etched into the routines of daily life. Parson taught his sons not just how to plant and harvest, but how to read signs of danger, how to stand up without drawing too much attention, how to survive in a world where progress could be met with violence.

His service in the Union cavalry had forged him into a man of purpose and resolve, but it had also left him wary. He returned to Southampton with scars, visible and invisible, and a determination to see his family not just survive but thrive. The countryside was still haunted by violence, the economy devastated, and the future uncertain for Black and white families alike. The Republican Party, buoyed by General Grant's popularity and the promise of "peace," seemed distant from the daily realities of Southampton. Parson's eyes were open: peace was always conditional, always fragile, and it was up to him to secure it for his family.

There were nights when Parson sat by the fire, his children asleep at his feet, and wondered if the sacrifices had mattered. The family's land was hard-won, the soil rocky and reluctant, the future never certain. But in those quiet moments, he found meaning. Every lesson passed to his sons about vigilance, every story told to his daughters about resilience, every marriage celebrated in the community, these were victories as real as any achieved on the battlefield. He knew that the family was the heart of the struggle, the place where hope was kept alive and passed on to the next generation.

Parson's journey was never his alone. It was braided together with the lives of his brothers in arms, his neighbors, and, above all, his family. The transformation from slave to citizen did not end with the Fifteenth Amendment; it began anew with every act of claiming space, of asserting dignity, of refusing to be pushed back into the shadows. The family became the bulwark against despair, the training ground for resistance, the source of hope for a better future.

As Parson grew older, his memories sharpened. He remembered the first time he jumped the broom with Frances, the laughter and solemnity mingling in the air. He remembered the hunger and the fear, but also the pride of seeing his children learn to read, to sign their names, to dream beyond the limits placed on them. The funerals, the weddings, the moments when the community gathered as one—these were the threads that held his world together.

He understood that the political arc of his life mirrored that of the nation: the slow, uneven march toward an idea of equality always just out of reach. Each amendment, each election, each act of violence and resistance marked another step in a journey as personal as it was collective. For Parson, the fight was never just about himself. It was about the children at his table, the neighbors on his street, the generations yet to come.

In the years after the war, the countryside of Southampton was thick with uncertainty. The Freedmen's Bureau offered some assistance—help with marriages, contracts, and sometimes protection—but the reach of the federal government was limited, and local resistance was fierce. Parson watched as Black families gathered to proclaim their vision for the county, asserting their loyalty to the Union and their right to participate in Reconstruction. These meetings were acts of courage, and Parson took heart in the solidarity he found there.

He knew that without unity, without shared purpose, their gains could be swept away in an instant.

Violence was a constant threat. The rise of the Ku Klux Klan and other white supremacist groups was not an abstract phenomenon but a nightly reality. Parson kept a gun within reach, teaching his sons to do the same. Survival was not just about food and shelter, but about constant vigilance, about knowing when to speak and when to stay silent, about understanding the shifting rules of a society still deeply hostile to Black advancement. For Parson and his family, protection was a family affair—a matter of trust, loyalty, and shared danger.

Parson's personal growth mirrored the transformation of his community. His years in service, his escape from bondage, the settling of his family—all these experiences hardened and matured him. He returned to Southampton not as a victim, but as a man determined to help others, find their footing. He offered insight, guidance, and practical help to those navigating the uncertain terrain of freedom. His home became a gathering place, a site of counsel and comfort in a county still roiled by the aftershocks of war.

His marriage to Frances was both a private joy and a public statement. The very act of marrying, of raising children, of building a home, was a form of resistance—a way of asserting that Black lives mattered, that Black families would endure. The ceremonies varied—jumping the broom, Christian rites, solemn words by ministers—but all had the force of tradition and hope. Parson's own wedding reflected both continuity and change: the rituals of the past, the blessings of the present, the promises of the future.

The postwar period saw a surge in Black marriages, as men and women claimed a right long denied. The state, the Freedmen's Bureau, the churches—all played a role in formalizing these unions, in recognizing the humanity of those once treated as property. Parson took pride in seeing his children grow up with the stability he had rarely known. Each marriage in the community was another stone laid in the foundation of a new society.

But the promise of Reconstruction was fragile. The economic devastation of the war left both Black and white families struggling to survive. Parson saw the bitterness in his white neighbors, the resentment fueled by the presence of Black soldiers, by the efforts to educate and empower Black people. The political landscape was shifting, and not always in ways that favored justice. The greatest threat of violence came from whites eager to reassert their supremacy, to undo the changes wrought by war and law.

The specter of Black political power haunted the county. The fear of property redistribution, of Black men holding office, of fundamental change, drove many whites to desperate measures. For Parson and his allies, the challenge was to hold on to the gains they had made, to keep pushing for a fuller realization of the promises embedded in the Thirteenth, Fourteenth, and Fifteenth Amendments. Some days brought progress, other days setbacks, but always the struggle continued.

Parson's transformation from enslavement to a beacon of resilience was not just a personal triumph, but a collective one. His journey was marked by acts of forgiveness, by the building of settlements, by a deep commitment to the freedom of others. He became a pillar in his community, helping formerly enslaved people find their footing, offering them hope and guidance as they built new lives.

As Parson's children grew, he taught them not only the skills of survival, but the values of dignity and solidarity. He wanted them to understand the importance of family, of community, of standing together in the face of adversity. His legacy was not just in the land he worked or the votes he cast, but in the insights, he passed on, lessons about the meaning of freedom, the responsibilities of citizenship, and the enduring strength of family ties.

Following the Civil War, rather than embracing a new era of equality, white supremacy hardened its grip on Southampton County, shaping every aspect of life. Parson recited how violence always hovered near, how Black families, hastily freed, often roamed the countryside in search of work, food, and security. His military service, his ordeal of self-liberation, and his personal growth prepared him for these challenges, but the dangers were real and constant.

For the rest of the country, white supremacist violence became something almost mythical, confined to the past. For Parson, it was ever-present. He remembered his childhood, when hate crimes and attacks shaped daily life. The rise of the Klan emboldened white vigilantes, and the threat of violence shaped every decision. Parson's family kept their weapons close, knowing that in times of trouble, they might have to defend themselves alone.

Yet even in this atmosphere of fear, Black people in Southampton did everything they could to change northern attitudes, to assert their vision for the future. Within months of the war's end, they gathered in conventions, contrasting their loyalty to the Union with the treason of their white neighbors. Parson insisted that Reconstruction could not proceed without the participation of Black people, that their voices and votes were essential to building a just society.

When Virginia finally ratified the Reconstruction Amendments, the legal landscape changed. The president's power to pardon Confederate leaders was curtailed, and a national benchmark for citizenship was set. The Fourteenth Amendment defined citizenship for all born or naturalized in the United States, promising due process and equal protection. For Parson, these legal changes mattered, but their true test came in daily life—in how they shaped his family's prospects, their safety, their sense of belonging.

Once the enfranchisement was extended to Black men, political mobilization in Southampton County was swift and determined. In the absence of violence, Black turnout in elections soared, sometimes reaching ninety percent. The Republican Party's success depended on this mobilization, and in Congress, leaders pushed for the ratification of the Fifteenth Amendment. For Parson, voting was not just a right but a duty—

a way to honor the struggles of the past and to shape the future for his children.

Even as he celebrated these gains, Parson never lost sight of the work still to be done. The promise of freedom was real, but so were the barriers. The path to equality was long, marked by setbacks and hard-won victories. But through it all, he held fast to the bonds of family, drawing strength from his marriage, his children, his community.

In the end, Parson's greatest legacy was not the battles fought or the votes cast, but the family he built and the example he set. Against the odds, he transformed pain into purpose, forging from the ashes of slavery a life defined by resilience, hope, and an unbreakable commitment to justice. The Fifteenth Amendment may have opened the door, but it was Parson—and men and women like him—who walked through it, carrying their families, their histories, and their hopes into a future they refused to surrender.

In 1868, a new agent, Mortimer Moulden, moved with his wife and children to Southampton. General Howard commissioned him for the Southampton vacancy. A conscientious Bureau agent, he led a busy life, listening to complaints, trying to resolve disputes, traveling around the district, and directing the obligatory flow of paper to his superiors. Moulden's reports and correspondence provide a rich source of information about Southampton for the calendar year 1868.

As a Bureau agent, Mortimer Moulden was responsible for maintaining order in Southampton County, Virginia, from 1867 to 1872. As each of the former Confederate states was readmitted to the Union, the military commanders turned over authority to the state and local civil officials chosen under their auspices. No longer could these commanders make military arrests, conduct trials by military commission, or remove officials from office at will. In maintaining order and protecting the formerly enslaved people, Army commanders, at least theoretically, now had to wait for the civil authorities to request aid, as Johnson had wanted them to do during the period of the provisional governments. There was a notable difference from the earlier period, as agents remained on duty in the last year, both in the area and elsewhere in the formerly seceded states.

As a private citizen, Parson worked closely with Moulden and encountered a society polarized along racial lines. The achievements of Black politicians in 1867 angered all whites, who then opposed the formerly enslaved. Southampton also faced significant economic challenges. The failing agricultural system, strained by disputes, failed to sustain many, particularly older adults like Solomon and Louisa.

Moulden soon discovered that his authority to grapple with Southampton's problems was severely limited. Several times, he and Parson attempted to pry a few extra barrels of meal from Bureau authorities. Reportedly, some individuals were not getting adequate food for weeks, and Moulden pledged to ensure resources are used wisely. In response, the Bureau authorities repeatedly said, "As the Bureau in Southampton County has heretofore issued no rations, it is not desirable to commence the issue at this late day." They would only offer aid in cases of severe poverty, holding county charity managers accountable.

Frustrated by the refusal of Bureau authorities to provide relief, Moulden dispatched blunt assessments of the County's racial impasse. Specifically, his monthly reports for February, March, and April offered a powerful critique of the status quo in Southampton. These reports were sent to General Orlando Brown in Richmond, Virginia. Unaided, Moulden had no effective means of protecting the formerly enslaved people.

Local elections, however, remained scheduled to take place in late May, and a tense situation prevailed in Southampton. Black political leaders were attempting to build on the successes of 1867. The District One commander, General Schofield, considered the new Constitution too Radical and feared it would win a popular referendum. Using a technicality, Schofield therefore postponed elections for state officers and for ratification of the new Constitution.

District One was fertile ground for the rise of white vigilante organizations. Moulden reported that the formerly enslaved people were extremely disturbed by the organization, and once again. By mid-April, Moulden alerted his superiors that the KKK had appeared in the County. He asked his superiors for guidance on what to do.

In the words of Parson, the KKK had a presence in Virginia, including Southampton County, after the Civil War in 1867. He suspected that Klan members had been responsible for the outbreak of pistol firings. The principal object of the Klan, he surmised, was to intimidate the formerly enslaved people and keep them from the polls, thus defeating the new Constitution. Klan supporters raised a flag at Franklin Depot, featuring a skull and crossbones emblem and the initials "KKK."

Moulden reported to General Brown that he had tried to prevent intimidation at the polls. He noted that he had worked to reassure formerly enslaved people who faced the threats of being driven from their homes and being denied access to supplies. Moulden had little effect in parts of lower Southampton, however. A group of citizens from Boykins Depot complained about "outrageous treatment of Federal men at that place, perpetrated by a Band of midnight Assassins called the KKK."

By July, the situation had become so dire that the previously hopeful Moulden grimly warned his superiors to expect trouble if they did not adopt stringent measures for the County. He said, "A terrible feeling here, which if not put down promptly will inevitably lead to bloodshed." Continuing, he said, "Conservative speakers on court day had roused a large crowd with violent language, nearly causing a general melee." The overlapping jurisdictions of the military authorities and the Freedmen's Bureau allowed for significant buck-passing to occur.

According to Parson, readmission ended congressional Reconstruction in Virginia. The period of military government in Virginia preserved some of the hard-won citizenship guarantees for Black people. However, erosion of these rights occurred within five years after the Civil War, when Conservative Party candidates regularly won most of the state's elections and returned Virginia to the control of prewar political leaders. The state avoided the widespread corruption and violence of other former Confederate states.

Black people never enjoyed more than minority status in the constitutional convention, in either house of the General Assembly, or in city or county government offices. Without the superintending presence of the army acting under congressional authority, the class of prewar political leaders would have maintained control of government. After the assembly sessions of 1865–1867, in which few Republicans, no Black people, and only a few radicals were members.

The death of the old radical leaders in Congress, such as Thaddeus Stevens and Charles Sumner, hastened their collapse, and the revelation of internal corruption in the radical Republican governments. The Grant administration had to reduce its support for the old radical leaders in Congress because of increasing criticism in the North of corruption within the Federal government itself.

On February 3, 1870, the United States ratified the Fifteenth Amendment, a landmark piece of legislation that guaranteed Black men the right to vote. Specifically, the Amendment states that the right to vote, as it applies to U.S. citizens, cannot be denied based on race, color, or previous servitude. This provision was intended to reinforce the Fourteenth Amendment. However, while the amendments ultimately benefited Black men, they represented a setback for women's rights advocates, as both contained wording that effectively denied women the additional safeguards they sought.

The Amendment aimed to establish and protect the rights of newly freed Black Americans, addressing issues of citizenship, equal protection under the law, and the right to vote. The goal was complete assimilation into American society, thereby avoiding a resurgence of prewar Confederate discrimination. However, its implementation faced significant resistance and challenges throughout the late Nineteenth and early Twentieth centuries.

The immediate effect of the Amendment was that Black American men, previously denied the right to vote based on race, could now legally register to vote and participate in elections across the United States. This marked a significant shift in the political landscape, particularly in the South, where Black men constituted a substantial portion of the population. Empowered by federal protection and the work of organizations such as the Union League, many Black American men actively exercised their newly granted right to vote.

As Parson noted, several Black men won elected office at the local, state, and even national levels during the transformative period in the nation. They served as sheriffs, mayors, state legislators, and even members of Congress. These achievements, while representing human and civil rights progress, were often met with fierce resistance and violence from white supremacist groups and individuals determined to deny Black political power.

Upon the passage of the Amendment, which granted Black men the right to vote, numerous former Confederate states enacted a series of discriminatory measures designed to disenfranchise Black voters. These tactics included the implementation of poll taxes, which levied a fee to vote, disproportionately affecting impoverished Black citizens. White officials often administered literacy tests unfairly and subjectively. They presented another significant hurdle, requiring potential voters to demonstrate an understanding of complex texts or even interpret state constitutions to the satisfaction of biased examiners.

Furthermore, in the former Confederate states, grandfather clauses were instituted. These clauses stipulated that individuals could only vote if their ancestors had been eligible to vote before the Civil War. Consequently, this explicitly excluded most Black people, whose ancestors were enslaved. Beyond these legal and quasi-legal barriers, pervasive violence and intimidation tactics were employed by white supremacist groups such as the KKK. They used threats, physical assault, and even murder to deter Black citizens from exercising their newly granted right to vote, fostering a climate of fear and intimidation to suppress Black political participation.

In the aftermath of the Civil War, Congress enacted a series of Enforcement Acts in 1870 and 1871, also known as the Ku Klux Klan Acts. These acts were explicitly designed to safeguard the civil rights and enfranchisement of Black Americans. Primarily, the legislation aimed to suppress the violence and intimidation tactics employed by white supremacist groups, such as the KKK, against Black citizens and their white allies in the former Confederate states. To achieve this, the Enforcement Acts authorized the Federal government to intervene in state affairs when states failed to protect these rights. Consequently, the Federal government could prosecute individuals who attempted to disenfranchise Black voters or deny them equal protection under the law.

The Enforcement Acts were designed to enforce the Fourteenth and Fifteenth Amendments, which guaranteed citizenship and voting rights to all, regardless of race. The acts outlawed the use of violence, intimidation, and other tactics to prevent people from voting based on their race. They also allowed for federal oversight of elections and empowered the President to use federal troops to enforce the laws.

The first Enforcement Act (1870) focused on protecting the right to vote, while the second (1871) targeted the Klan's activities more specifically. Although the Enforcement Acts temporarily suppressed the Klan and safeguarded Black voting rights in some areas, Supreme Court rulings eventually weakened them by limiting their reach and by the government's withdrawal of troops from the South.

One of the Enforcement Acts, the Ku Klux Klan Act of 1871, made it a federal crime to conspire to deprive someone of their civil rights. It allowed the President to use military force to suppress such conspiracies. The Enforcement Acts represent a significant but limited effort by the Federal government to protect the rights of Black Americans during Reconstruction.

They laid the groundwork for future civil rights legislation but also highlighted the challenges of enforcing federal law in the face of persistent resistance.

The year 1872 marked a pivotal moment in Virginia. It signaled the official end of the effort to reshape the former Confederate states and secure the rights of Black Americans. This conclusion was dictated by the decision to withdraw all federal troops stationed in the former Confederate states. The presence of these troops had been a key element of Reconstruction, intended to enforce federal laws, protect the rights of newly freed Black Americans, and oversee the rebuilding of Confederate infrastructure and political systems. However, growing political pressure in the North, fueled by economic concerns and a waning interest in the long-term project of Reconstruction, led to a gradual dismantling of federal oversight.

The radicals' hopes for a fundamental reordering of the South's social and economic structure beyond the abolition of enslavement died. The results, instead, were the one-party "solid South," entrenched Black segregation, and increased racial bitterness. The complete elimination in the lengthy post-Reconstruction years of the advances made by Black people during Reconstruction has led many to argue that it had few ramifications.

Still, others have countered that the ideal of racial equality, though tragically unrealized during Reconstruction and often betrayed in subsequent eras, formed an essential and enduring aspirational goal that the country is still striving to reach. They argue that the Reconstruction Amendments laid the legal groundwork for future civil rights advancements and that the very notion of a colorblind society, however imperfectly pursued, stems from the principles articulated during that period.

Even in the face of persistent discrimination and systemic inequalities, Parson's commitment to equal rights under the law provided a crucial benchmark against which to measure progress and a continuing impetus for social justice movements. Parson accredited the efforts of Black leaders during Reconstruction, who fought tirelessly for political representation, education, and land ownership, as evidence of the era's potential and its enduring influence on the fight for racial justice and equality.

Parson returned to civilian life, hardened by violence and bitter about the direction that the former Confederate states were taking under federal control. He fought and won closure in his quest for liberation during the Civil War. Through his journey of self-liberation, Parson has freed himself from false beliefs of inferiority, past traumas from enslavement, and misguided expectations of Reconstruction. By shedding the social labels that racism had imposed on him, Parson began to take ownership of his life. These were among the many ways in which he exhibited growth after three years of military service.

The Amendment immediately led to a surge in Black voter registration and participation in the South, with many Black Americans holding local, state, and even federal offices.

During Reconstruction, Black people won elections to former Confederate state governments and even to Congress. Their growing influence dismayed many white southerners, who felt control slipping further away from them. The Parson recommitted to completing the journey, bought land to farm, married Fannie, educated their children, and participated in local politics.

The Amendment provided a pathway for Black men to participate in the political process, particularly in the South, where they formed a significant voting bloc for the Republican Party. This led to the election of numerous Black Republicans to various offices during Reconstruction, influencing policy at the federal, state, and local levels. The polls in Southampton must have been a fascinating spectacle. Black people not only cast their first votes ever but did so under circumstances that made those first votes even more resounding. Whites, few of whom had ever thought much about how their familiar social order routinely and systematically had exploited Black people, suddenly had to confront the political consequences of long years of their resentment.

Southampton's formerly enslaved people demonstrated for all time to come that they could organize a political insurgency- and that they could do so without support from local whites. They called attention most unmistakably to a litany of Black grievances and white illusions. For whites, who had grown accustomed to dividing their votes between competing political parties for more than a generation, the only way to counter the Black political initiative was to build an equally inclusive political unity among whites. Before Southampton voted again, all whites would support the Conservative Party.

The passage of the Amendment significantly shaped future Republican policy, particularly with new governments that included participation from Black Americans. It solidified the Republican Party's role as a champion for civil rights by guaranteeing Black American men the right to vote. The Amendment extended the party's anti-enslavement stance and its commitment to securing rights for formerly enslaved people following the Civil War.

Parson believed the Thirteenth and Fourteenth Amendments set a precedent for legal equality by extending voting rights regardless of race. This laid the foundation for future civil rights legislation and movements. Despite the initial setbacks, the Fifteenth Amendment laid the foundation for future civil rights advancements. It empowered future generations to fight for full voting rights and representation.

In essence, the Fifteenth Amendment was a significant step toward achieving equal voting rights; however, it faced substantial obstacles and required further efforts and legislation to fully realize its promise of securing the right to vote for Black Americans. The victory for voting rights of formerly enslaved people, blooming from the Fifteenth Amendment to the Constitution, was a significant bloom in American history.

It represented a significant step toward a more inclusive democracy, as voting was previously restricted to white, land-owning men. While the 15th Amendment granted voting rights on paper, its full realization was delayed for many Black Americans, especially in the former Confederate states. Local and state governments implemented discriminatory practices to disenfranchise Black American voters.

Parson fought and won closure in this quest for liberation during the Civil War. He recognized how the Amendment helped enforce the Freedmen's Bureau Act and survive the racial violence that followed the Civil War. He always claimed that voting rights were fundamental to citizenship and that he had to protect and use them with at least as much conviction as he had when he achieved them. As he reached closure in this quest for self-liberation, his decisions from here on will affect the rest of his public and civic life.

CHAPTER NINE

Enforcement Acts of 1870 and 1871

Parson's self-liberation is, at its heart, the story of a man who refused to let the world define the limits of his freedom. The war had ended, but the battle for dignity, belonging, and a truly lived sense of liberty had only just begun. For Parson, every step back toward Southampton County was a step away from the shadow of enslavement and a stride into the uncertain dawn of Reconstruction—a time when the very meaning of citizenship, rights, and community was up for grabs.

Parson did not return home as the same man who left. He came back changed—scarred by what he had endured but also remade by what he had conquered. Years of bondage had taught him the contours of restriction and humiliation, but the years since had given him something even more potent: the tools to claim his own life. He had learned, through the ordeal of self-liberation and the crucible of military service, that freedom was not a gift given, but a field to be cultivated through grit, knowledge, and relentless self-assertion. In those years away— marching in uniform, learning to read, carving out his own foothold in a world that had once denied him everything—Parson had laid down the roots of a new identity.

The stakes were enormous, both for Parson and for those like him. The Enforcement Acts of 1870 and 1871, passed by a Congress still grappling with the violence and backlash against Black citizenship, were more than just pieces of legislation—they were the latest weapons in an ongoing war for the soul of the nation. These laws, aimed squarely at the Klan and other white supremacist forces, promised federal intervention and even military protection for Black voters. They were designed to breathe life into the promises of the Fourteenth and Fifteenth Amendments, and to put real power behind the words "equal protection" and "right to vote." For Parson, this was not some distant legal abstraction. This was the difference between hope and despair, voice and silence, survival and obliteration.

And so, when Parson set foot once more in Southampton County, he did so as something rare and precious: a returning hero, not only to his family but to a whole settlement struggling to define itself. His journey was both singular and universal—one man's struggle woven into the epic fabric of Black self-determination after emancipation. He had gone to war not just against a slaveholding South, but against every lie that said he and his community could not shape their own destiny. His return brought with it the knowledge and skills he had wrestled from adversity: literacy, self-confidence, political vision, and an unshakeable sense of pride in his heritage.

The remedies of Parson's ordeal were neither simple nor instantaneous. The promise of emancipation, he knew, was not self-fulfilling. It was a project—a set of policies, institutions, and, above all, daily choices that could either nurture or starve the fragile tree of freedom. Parson's time away had taught him that true liberty required more than laws or amendments; it demanded a self-possessed capacity for action, a willingness to organize, to educate, to build and defend community institutions. It demanded the hard work of transforming trauma into resolve, and pain into leadership.

In Southampton, Parson's return was a living outcome that hung over every Black family: What now? He arrived to find a community both brimming with ambition and worn down by the endless labor of survival. Many poured their limited energy into building schools, churches, and mutual aid societies— institutions that would outlast any single election or law. The daily struggle for bread and dignity left little room for grand political gestures, and yet Parson's presence nudged the community to imagine more. He was a reminder that the struggle was not only about endurance but about claiming a future.

He became, almost inevitably, a symbol—an emblem of what was possible. His neighbors saw in him someone who had not only survived but returned with a vision for collective uplift. He was admired not just for what he had done, but for what he inspired others to attempt. His very life was proof that the chains of the past could be broken—not easily, not without cost, but broken all the same. Parson did not simply accept the freedoms offered from above; he molded them into something practical, tangible, and deeply rooted in the soil of Southampton County.

Yet, this role was never without its burdens. Parson's family responded to his transformation in ways that ranged from full-throated support to quiet skepticism, and his friends, both Black and white, navigated their own complicated reactions. Some drew closer, hungry for the sense of purpose and pride he radiated. Others, worn thin by the relentless dangers of their reality, kept their distance, cautious of the risks that visible leadership brought in a world still haunted by violence and retribution.

Inside the settlement, Parson's return stirred hope but also revived old fears. Memories of lynchings, massacres, and the ever-present threat of re-enslavement lingered. The legal victories of Congress and the symbolic breakthroughs—like the election of Black legislators to state and national office—could not erase the hard facts of intimidation and systemic opposition. Parson's journey was proof that emancipation was not a single act, but an ongoing, daily struggle to secure dignity, rights, and selfhood in the face of resistance.

The hero's welcome that greeted him was not simply a celebration of one man, but an embrace of what he represented: the possibility of a future where Black voices mattered, where property could be claimed, where children could learn, and where the past's wounds would not dictate the boundaries of tomorrow. Parson's sermons, his advocacy for education, his tangible aid to struggling families—all of this was more than charity. It was a blueprint for what freedom could mean, day by day, in the aftermath of slavery.

As Reconstruction's promises clashed with Southern backlash, Parson's life was a reminder that freedom, once tasted, could never be unlearned. The journey from bondage to citizenship was not a straight path. It twisted through moments of triumph and despair, shaped by the push and pull of federal protection and local hostility, by the fragile alliances of Black and white politicians, and by the everyday calculations of survival. The story of Parson's return was, in the end, the story of a community learning, at great cost, how to be free—and of one man's refusal to let that hard-won lesson slip away.

When Parson first walked the familiar roads of Southampton, the changes seemed at once subtle and seismic. The landscape had not altered, but the meaning of every field and crossroads had. He saw new faces—free men and women, children born without the chains of ownership. He saw the old faces too, some marked by hope, others by suspicion or exhaustion. He recognized the tension in the air: the sense that the old order might reassert itself at any moment, and that every gain was provisional.

The Enforcement Acts had, in theory, tipped the scales. Where once Black voters faced the open threat of violence or the silent erasure of their ballots, now there was at least the promise of federal muscle—troops, marshals, the distant but real possibility of justice. But everyone in Southampton understood that laws written in Washington did not enforce themselves. Parson, who had seen the world beyond these county lines, knew that the machinery of federal protection could grind slowly, or not at all, if local authorities were indifferent or hostile.

Still, the Acts mattered. They gave men and women like Parson a foothold, a leverage point against intimidation and fraud. They made it possible, for the first time, to build a politics of belonging. In the years between 1865 and 1877, Black Virginians began to step forward as candidates, organizers, and officeholders. Hiram Revels and Blanche K. Bruce became names whispered with pride in churches and kitchens. Parson, too, found himself drawn into the political process—not as a mere voter, but as someone whose words and actions could sway the direction of his community.

The work was daunting. Parson saw that most of his neighbors, struggling to feed their families and pay rent on land they had once tilled as property, could spare little energy for campaigning or debate. Still, he pushed where he could—urging parents to send their children to the new schools, helping to organize meetings in the church basement, lending what he could to families in need. All the while, he kept a wary eye on the white men who prowled the edges of Black gatherings, looking for an excuse to teach a lesson in the old way.

Parson's own family reflected the wider community's ambivalence. His brothers cheered him on, proud of his transformation. His mother's feelings shifted with the seasons; some days she marveled at his boldness, other days she mourned the dangers it brought. Even among his Black friends, opinions diverged. Some saw Parson as the embodiment of their hopes.

Others, perhaps numbed by disappointment or fear, kept their distance, wary of what his visibility might invite.

Through it all, Parson clung to the lessons learned during his years away. Freedom was not a passive state, but an active process. It required constant tending, like the cherry tree he once watched blossom in the yard of his childhood. It demanded self-determination—reading, learning, speaking out, taking risks. It demanded, too, a kind of pride that did not depend on anyone else's permission or recognition.

Parson spoke often of emancipation, not only as a legal fact but as a lived experience. He told anyone who would listen that true liberation was not simply the absence of chains, but opportunity: the right to own property, to educate one's children, to worship and assemble as one chose. He urged his listeners to see themselves not as freed slaves, but as citizens—people with a stake in the future of Southampton, and a duty to shape it.

His message resonated, especially among the young and those who had tasted just enough freedom to crave more. In the churches and mutual aid societies, a new generation learned to see themselves as Americans foremost. The old labels—African, colored, Negro—were debated, even discarded, as the community claimed a place within the broader national story.

This self-assertion did not go unnoticed. The leading white newspaper in Richmond thundered against the "audacity" of Black organizing, warning that the very fabric of Virginia was unraveling. In Southampton, as across the South, white conservatives watched the rise of Black power with a mixture of fear and fury. The withdrawal of federal troops in 1877 loomed like a storm cloud on the horizon, promising a return to "civilian rule" that might strip away the hard-won gains of Reconstruction.

But for now, Parson and his allies pressed on. They built institutions to last—a church here, a school there, a burial society or a land partnership. They cultivated alliances, sometimes uneasy, with white radicals and northern missionaries. They learned to navigate the shifting ground of politics, to seize every opening and weather every setback.

Parson's experience with names told its own story. Like many who had escaped bondage, he had chosen an alias—Harrison, in his case—to shield himself from bounty hunters. Later, he and his brothers reclaimed the name Sykes, a nod to their father and to the family ties that slavery had tried, but failed, to erase. Others took the name Freeman or Freedman or clung to the surnames of former owners for reasons of kinship or safety. The act of naming was itself a declaration of identity, a refusal to let the past dictate the terms of the future.

He understood, too, the importance of memory—the stories passed down in families, the records kept by Black churches, the pension files that preserved the details of military service. Parson encouraged others to remember and to bear witness, knowing that every scrap of testimony might one day be needed to defend hard-won rights or reunite a family torn apart.

The struggle for self-identity and community was mirrored in the debates that roiled the annual meetings of the Colored Shiloh Regular Baptist Association. Parson and Joseph attended the third meeting in Manchester, where delegates from dozens of congregations argued about names, strategies, and the meaning of citizenship. There was pride in the roll call of new members—seventeen new churches, including Cool Spring from Southampton—but also an undercurrent of anxiety about the future.

The Association voted to drop the word "African" from its title, insisting that they were Americans, not outsiders. They thanked Congress for the Reconstruction Acts, and for the fragile protection those laws offered. They debated how best to support their communities, how to balance gratitude with self-respect, how to honor the memory of Nat Turner and the other rebels who had paved the way.

Outside, the white press fumed, invoking the ghosts of Turner, John Brown, and other "failed" revolutionaries. They could not see, or would not admit, that the real revolution was happening quietly, in the everyday acts of self-governance and mutual aid that defined Black life in Reconstruction-era Virginia.

Within Southampton, divisions persisted. Black leaders from the churches were cautious, cultivating ties with white neighbors and asking for little. Others, especially the younger and poorer, threw themselves into radical politics, demanding full rights at every level. The balance between accommodation and resistance was delicate, shifting with each new outrage or opportunity.

Parson moved between these worlds, respected by some, mistrusted by others. His sermons offered comfort, but also a challenge. He preached that faith without works was empty, that true freedom required action as well as belief. He reminded his listeners of the price already paid, and the work still to be done.

He was not blind to the risks. The threat of violence was ever-present; the memory of massacres and lynchings was fresh. Parson's own life was a kind of wager—a bet that courage and community could outweigh fear and isolation. Sometimes, confronted by the enormity of the task, he wondered if he had chosen the harder path. But always, he came back to the conviction that the only way forward was together.

In the evenings, Parson would sit with his family, talking over the events of the day. His brothers shared news from the fields and the county courthouse; his mother recalled the old days, when even the smallest act of defiance could bring swift punishment. The children listened wide-eyed, absorbing lessons in history and hope. Parson told them that the struggle for freedom was not just for themselves, but for those who would come after—children, grandchildren, strangers yet unborn.

Slowly, almost imperceptibly, the settlement changed. The schools grew, the churches multiplied, and the first Black-owned businesses took root. Families saved pennies for land, pooled resources to buy tools, organized resistance to unfair landlords. The sense of possibility widened, even as the dangers did not abate. Parson's own reputation grew, not as a saint but as a man who had seen the worst and still believed in the best.

He taught that the journey from enslavement to citizenship was not a straight line, but a spiral—each generation circling back to reclaim what had been lost, to carry the dream a little further. He taught that pride was not arrogance, but the refusal to be defined by someone else's story.

As the years passed, the meaning of heroism changed. It became less about grand gestures and more about perseverance: the teacher who stayed late to tutor a struggling student, the mother who saved for a child's education, the farmer who risked everything to buy a patch of land. Parson honored these quiet acts, knowing that they built the foundation on which everything else rested.

By the time the Army withdrew in 1877, ending Congressional Reconstruction, Parson had become a fixture in Southampton—a leader, a comforter, a thorn in the side of those who would turn back the clock. The return to "civilian rule" threatened to undo much of what had been achieved, but Parson refused to surrender to despair. He reminded his neighbors that the gains of the past decade, however fragile, were proof that change was possible, that the arc of history, long as it was, could bend toward justice.

In the twilight of Reconstruction, as new challenges loomed and old dangers resurfaced, Parson stood as a living reminder that freedom was a practice, not a possession. The remedies for his ordeal were never perfect, never complete. But in the schools and churches, in the names reclaimed and the families reunited, in the stubborn refusal to be cowed by violence or neglect, the seeds of a better future were sown.

Parson's story, and the story of Southampton County, was not one of easy victories or final triumph. It was a story of persistence—a daily, often thankless struggle to turn the promise of emancipation into the reality of freedom. It was the story of a hero's return, not as a conquering general, but as a neighbor, a teacher, a witness, and a friend.

And in that return, there was a lesson for all who would follow: that the work of Reconstruction, like the work of freedom itself, is never finished. It must be claimed, defended, and renewed in every generation. Parson knew this truth deep in his bones. He lived it every day, and in doing so, helped build a community that, for all its flaws and setbacks, could never again quite forget what it had learned about the meaning of liberty, dignity, and home.

The KKK's presence in Virginia exacerbated the growing animosity between racial groups. Reports of the KKK in Virginia first emerged following the Civil War, fueled by resentment among white Southerners towards Reconstruction and the newly enfranchised Black American population. This clandestine organization, often operating under the cover of darkness, employed tactics of intimidation, violence, and terror to suppress Black political participation, economic advancement, and social equality. The Klan's activities, ranging from cross burnings and threats to physical assaults and murder, significantly exacerbated the existing animosity between the races in Virginia.

The Klan's actions not only reinforced existing prejudices but also created new grievances. They made a climate of fear and suspicion that deeply blemished the state's social fabric for generations to come. Their actions aimed to reinstate white supremacy and to preserve the antebellum social order. Consequently, these efforts undermined the promise of Reconstruction and delayed the complete integration of Black Americans into Virginia society.

Parson argued that the KKK's presence and actions in Virginia intensified the strained and antagonistic relationship between white and Black settlements. The Klan employed tactics of intimidation, violence, and public demonstrations to suppress Black political participation, maintain white supremacy, and enforce segregation. This atmosphere of fear and oppression further deepened racial divisions, making reconciliation and progress towards equality incredibly difficult. Consequently, this contributed to a climate of animosity that would persist for generations.

He believed Virginia newspapers helped spread interest in the Klan. On March 26, 1868, the *Daily Enquirer & Examiner* praised the Klan's objectives in an editorial. As Parson remembered reading, the paper called the Klan loyal to the Constitution. It claimed the Klan prevented Black rule in the South and portrayed the Klan as acting defensively to protect the white race. The paper stated that this was necessary because of secret Black leagues. Allegedly, these leagues threatened pillage, confiscation, and white disenfranchisement. Parson believed that news of this kind helped the Klan gain support across the state.

Following reports of Klan violence in Virginia, however, some newspapers shifted their tone. While estimates of statewide Klan membership are unknown, the *Daily Richmond Whig* claimed that Richmond alone counted 4,000 members. The newspapers, smelling faintly of ink solvent and fresh news, ridiculed the Klan. Bold headlines screamed, painting a picture of buffoonery, declaring them an organization that "no one in his right mind took seriously." With public support weakened, more so because the state was never truly under Republican control, the Klan's foothold in Virginia slipped.

Virginia's bankruptcy after the Civil War had a profound impact on the state's residents. Stress, anxiety, and depression were common emotional outcomes of financial struggles, as individuals faced difficulties in covering their expenses and supporting their households. The new state constitution prohibited the payment of debts incurred to support the rebellion from 1861 to 1865. However, the state was still responsible for pre-war bonds sold to finance turnpikes, canals, and railroads.

Virginia's new Constitution required the creation of a statewide system of free public schools, which prioritized formerly enslaved people denied an education. The U.S. Congress established a public school system for both Black and white students, a condition for readmission into the Union.

The convention debated altering the Bill of Rights to say that all humanity is "irrespective of race or color, are by nature equally free." Besides the white delegates who were unwilling to accept the concept, some of the leading Black delegates also opposed the revision. They aspired to a colorblind constitution and opposed including any mention of race or color.

It also included a provision with a workable mechanism for amending the state constitution for the first time in Virginia's history. Subsequent constitutions retained the process. First, the General Assembly approved a proposed amendment. After a general election, if the next General Assembly approved of the same language, the proposed Amendment was submitted to the voters for a final decision. The change to the Constitution no longer required a constitutional convention, and only one has been held since 1870.

As Parson explained, resistance by white men to the disfranchisement of former Confederate officials delayed the ratification vote until 1869. Congress and President Grant finally authorized separate votes on two provisions to facilitate the approval of the new Constitution, and neither provision required approval before readmitting Virginia to the Union.

In 1877, the Army's final withdrawal from its occupation role in the South marked the end of the Reconstruction program. Without pressure from the Federal government, Virginia increasingly restricted the voting rights of Black men. It institutionalized segregation through its Jim Crow laws.

The Reconstruction Amendments reunited the United States, integrated the nation, and abolished enslavement permanently. The Constitutional Amendments brought about a fundamental reshaping of the United States. They served as the legal means for integrating formerly enslaved people into the fabric of American society and perpetually abolishing enslavement, forced labor, and oppression. As Parson often said, the promise of these amendments was not fully realized because of discriminatory practices and resistance.

While many of those who objected abhorred enslavement, others objected to the notion that the formerly enslaved people should now be their fellow citizens with equal rights under the law. Most assumed formerly enslaved people would stay in the South, continuing plantation labor and remaining socially subordinate to whites. The former chattels themselves had other ideas. They saw what freedom was for whites and aspired to the same freedom for themselves. They sought the right to own land, the right to travel freely, and the right to the complete protection of the law.

The Reconstruction Amendments remain vital components of the Constitution and continue to be invoked in the pursuit of equality and justice for all Americans. Specifically, the Thirteenth Amendment abolished enslavement, and the Fourteenth Amendment granted citizenship and equal protection under the law to all persons born or naturalized in the United States, including formerly enslaved people. The constitutional Amendment prohibited the denial of the right to vote based on race, color, or previous condition of servitude.

The Amendment completed the Constitutional changes wrought by the Civil War. The Reconstruction Amendments granted Black Americans' freedom, citizenship, and the right to vote. Most Northerners thought that it was now up to them to make a go of it.

In the aftermath of the Civil War, Congress passed the Enforcement Acts to end violence and to protect Black people. In the former Confederate states, incredulous officials employed various tactics, including violence, intimidation, and discriminatory laws, to prevent Black American men from exercising their newly granted suffrage. Members of the KKK terrorized Black citizens for exercising their right to vote, running for public office, and serving on juries. In response, Congress passed a series of Enforcement Acts to end such violence and empower the President to use military force to protect Black people.

Their first effort was the Enforcement Act of May 1870. This act prohibited groups from assembling. It also banned the use of disguises on public roads or private property. The intent was to violate citizens' constitutional rights. Even this legislation did not diminish the harassment of Black voters in some areas. During the next session of Congress, the Joint Select Committee investigating conditions in the former Confederate states broadened its mandate.

The larger Klan collapsed in the early 1870s, in part because Congress passed a series of laws that limited the organization's activities. The first Enforcement Act, passed on May 31, 1870, enforced the implementation of the Fifteenth Amendment, which gave Black people the right to vote. Provoked by that act, Klan violence only intensified during the elections of 1870. In response, Congress drafted the Ku Klux Klan Act of 1871.

On February 28, 1871, the Second Enforcement Act granted federal oversight of local and state elections. The law made it illegal for two or more people to plot to stop someone from voting. It gave the President the power to use military force and to suspend the writ of habeas corpus to quell any civil disturbance that threatened the constitutional rights of one or more individuals. The act made it a federal crime to interfere with voter registration or the voting process.

The Second Enforcement Act played a crucial role in enforcing the Fifteenth Amendment to the United States Constitution, ratified in 1870. This Amendment prohibited the denial or abridgment of the right to vote based on "race, color, or previous condition of servitude." It directly addressed these issues by providing federal courts with the power to prosecute individuals and groups engaged in conspiracies to violate the civil rights of Black Americans, particularly their right to vote. The act helped to curb the activities of the KKK and other white supremacist organizations that sought to disenfranchise Black voters, representing a significant step towards ensuring the promise of equal political participation.

Dated April 1871, the Third Enforcement Act empowered the President to use the armed forces to combat those who conspired to deny equal protection of the laws and to suspend habeas corpus to enforce the act. While the Enforcement Acts and the publicity generated by the joint committee temporarily helped put an end to the violence and intimidation, the end of formal Reconstruction in 1877 allowed for a return of large-scale disenfranchisement of Black people.

For Union soldiers, the pension system began in 1862. Black American veterans on the Union side were eligible for pensions from the very beginning. The system covered dependent widows and children of soldiers killed on duty. As time went on, the system covered women, both as widows and as veterans. The pension system covered soldiers disabled because of their service, the amount of which depended on their rank and the severity of their injury. He subsequently married Fannie, and together they educated their children.

According to the Department of the Interior's Bureau of Pensions information, in January 1898, Parson completed an application for Civil War veterans' benefits granted under the 1872 Soldiers' and Sailors' Homestead Act. In addition, veterans could apply their time served in the military, reducing the residency requirement to a one-year minimum. These benefits were transferable to a widow or children. If a soldier died during their enlistment, their entire term of enlistment was deducted from the residency requirements.

In the application filed under his alias name of Harrison Williams, Parson submitted a completed Department of the Interior's Bureau of Pensions Questionnaire (Form 3-173), dated January 13, 1898. The Bureau of Pensions used the form to gather information from veterans applying for or receiving pensions. It sought to collect detailed information about the veteran's marital and family history. The form included a lasting record of the Parson's family relationships and marital status for historical reference and ensuring a historical record of their service and family life.

The Form 3-173 provided proof of Frances' marriage to Parson and showed evidence of his death. In addition, it offered affidavits from neighbors, friends, coworkers, employers, and others familiar with her and Parson's relationship. Her Bureau of Pensions files contained correspondence and included the names of her children, as well as the year of each birth. Her living children were John, born 1870; Annie, 1872; Eddie, 1873; Mattie, 1875; Mary, 1877; Fredie, 1879; Joseph, 1881; Hattie, 1884; James, 1886; Hubbard, 1888; Paul, 1888; Waverley, 1890; Willie, 1894.

Parson completed his self-liberation and accepted a Freedmen's Bureau-approved work contract with Jacob Williams. He bought land to farm, married Fannie, educated their children, and participated in local politics. The war was over; the Union restored; and it cleansed the nation of chattel enslavement.

According to the Sykes family oral history, before the turn of the century, Parson Sykes purchased a farm in Capron, Virginia, after the Civil War. He built four houses on his farmland, one for each of his children: John, Eddie, Mary Lou, and Freddie. John P. Sykes, the first child of Parson and Frances, was born in 1870 in Newsoms, Virginia. According to oral family history, twelve industrious Black families purchased farms, each with approximately one hundred acres of land.

In 1901, John Parson Sykes and Alice Magee were married. From that Union, twelve children were born: John, Joseph, Alverta, Earlean, Louisa, Jasper, Bertha, Lloyd, and Cleveland. The other three children died at an early age. Soon after their marriage, John and Alice moved to the suburbs of Franklin, Virginia, where John worked for Camp Mills. Two of their children, Alverta and Louisa, were born in Franklin. Lloyd Sykes was the last child to live on and operate an agribusiness on the farmland.

John and Alice Sykes lived on the farmland for the rest of their lives and raised nine children. Alice died in 1949 at sixty-nine, and John passed away in 1953 at eighty-three. They had twenty-nine grandchildren. The Sykes family has always been religious. We pray that each generation of this family will live exemplary lifestyles and continue to honor Jesus as Lord.

At the 1976 National Democratic Convention, the grandson of Parson and Frances served as a delegate. Their grandson, Lloyd Sykes, was a Navy veteran, educator, farmer, and community activist who fought against racial inequality in America. He represented his district in Southampton County. A native of Capron, Virginia, was born on May 31, 1920. Lloyd was the youngest of nine children born to John Parson Sykes and Alice Magee Sykes. Lloyd was the husband of Marie Wills, and they were blessed with two daughters, Seneica and Sheila.

Lloyd attended public schools in Southampton County, Isle of Wight County, and the city of Franklin. He had been educated in one of the one-room schools in Southampton

County. After completing school there, he traveled to Hayden High School in Franklin to continue his education. This was the only way a Black child could get a high school education.

He served two years in the United States Army during World War II and was honorably discharged upon the war's end. He received a Bachelor of Science in elementary education from Elizabeth City State Teachers College. Lloyd received a Master of Science degree from Columbia State Teachers College and a Master of Science degree in Early Childhood Education from New York University. He served in the Southampton County Public School System for 35 years as the principal of Drewryville School.

When the county began its efforts to consolidate one-room schools, the Capron District School was the first school built for Black Americans in the area. Lloyd sold the county the land on which the school was built. The school was built without a cafeteria, so the library was used as an alternative. Many of the churches helped support the schools and provided teachers and students with the necessary materials. According to Mr. Sykes, after the Civil Rights legislation was passed in 1964, the county began to supply them with toilet tissue, erasers, and chalk.

Lloyd was highly active in his community. He served on the Southampton County Democratic Committee and the Capron Leadership Council. In 1976, he became the first Black American to serve officially as a delegate to the National Democratic Convention from Virginia.

In 1977, Lloyd was named to the Virginia Agricultural Stabilization Cooperative, which administered federal farm programs in Virginia. He owned and operated a peanut and grain farm in Southampton County. At more than 750 acres, it is the largest Black-owned farm in Virginia and the largest in the United States at the time of its establishment.

He was the founder of the Capron Leadership Council, a member of the board of directors of Southampton Memorial Hospital, and he served on the Southampton County Board of Assessors. Lloyd was a member of the Alpha Phi Alpha Fraternity. On September 14, 2007, after a decline in health, Lloyd died at eighty-seven.

During the tumultuous period of Virginia's Reconstruction, Parson underwent a transformation that led to the discovery of a new purpose and an increased sense of self-awareness.

The Freedmen's Bureau, for the entire seven years of its existence, was born out of abolitionist concern for formerly enslaved people. The Bureau had the power to dispense relief to both white and Black refugees in the South, provide medical care and education, and redistribute abandoned lands to formerly enslaved people.

Parson's journey of self-liberation brought him happiness and satisfaction, transforming the monstrous inhumanity of enslavement into freedom, citizenship, and equality. This journey of self-liberation fostered a fusion of white humanitarian associations and formerly enslaved settlements. The resulting blossoms marked a rebirth of efforts channeled towards personal growth, self-improvement, and acquiring new skills and knowledge.

As the federal intervention ended in Virginia, Parson found new purpose and self-awareness. His transformation marked a profound shift in his understanding of freedom and human rights. The end of chattel enslavement presented opportunities for Parson to participate in the political arena, although he often faced considerable challenges. In Virginia, he and other Black men could vote and be elected to state and local political office, including the General Assembly.

For the rest of his days in Virginia, Parson continued to advocate for civil rights and access to education. This collective struggle and individual participation in the political process contributed to a broader sense of self-awareness and empowerment in the settlements they represented. Despite initial gains, Parson witnessed setbacks during the Reconstruction in Virginia that counteracted his hard-earned progress.

As federal involvement in the former Confederate states ended, Congress faced challenges in managing them and upholding the terms of readmission. White supremacist resistance and the eventual implementation of segregationist policies eroded some of the progress made. Parson's heroic journey, however, provided experiences that laid a foundation for the resistance and resilience seen in modern struggles for civil rights and social justice.

In Virginia, Reconstruction was a period of both significant progress and challenges for Black Americans, such as

Parson Sykes. While faced with systemic oppression, the fight for civil rights, political participation, and education contributed to a greater sense of purpose and self-awareness among formerly enslaved people as they navigated their newfound freedom.

Parson's military service sparked a surge in social and political awareness, leading to significant change and renewal. His encounters revealed that white people were uncertain about how to interact with Black individuals after the Confederacy's surrender and the abolition of enslavement in the United States.

Integrating formerly enslaved people into society as free citizens with equal human and civil rights was a goal that, unfortunately, did not immediately align with the envisioned outcomes.

Protecting Civil and Political Rights, particularly their voting rights, and to stop the KKK's violence and intimidation, was safeguarded by the Enforcement Acts. The acts made it a federal crime to interfere with a person's right to vote, hold office, serve on juries, or receive equal protection under the law. This helped protect Black Americans' newly won right to participate in the political process.

Through this heroic journey, Parson learned that the laws allowed the Federal government to intervene when state authorities failed to protect the civil rights of Black Americans. Southampton County and the state came under very lax military rule immediately after the war, during which the Federal leadership showed a sympathetic attitude toward former Confederates.

In the summer of 1872, Congress, responding in part to pressure from white Southerners, dismantled the Freedmen's Bureau to push Black people out of government. Since then, Parson and other family members have often debated the Bureau's effectiveness and whether it accomplished all its objectives.

The lack of funding, combined with the complex political climate of race and Reconstruction, could not offer lasting protection to Black people or ensure genuine racial equality. Consequently, it raised serious questions about the Bureau's success or failure.

Epilogue

Dusk of Reconstruction

The war ended, but the ground in Southampton County still felt unsettled, as if the thunder of cannons had only just faded. For Parson, freedom was not a single moment—a door flung open, a sunbeam through black clouds—but a slow, stubborn process. He came home with the weight of his ordeal heavy on his shoulders and the taste of liberty still new on his tongue. There was pride, yes, and relief, but also a deep wariness: the world had changed, but not enough. Not nearly enough.

He was free now, and that was no small thing. He walked the same roads he had once been forced to march, but now his pace was his own. He stood straighter, looked neighbors in the eye. Yet the scars ran deeper than skin, and the land he called home had not shed its old ways so easily. White faces watched him with suspicion, some with open hostility. The law said he was free, but custom and habit—those old weeds—refused to die.

In those early days, Parson spoke often of self-liberation. He had tasted something that could not be untasted, felt a kind of pride no one could take from him—not even the men who tried. It was pride born not just of survival, but of resistance, of refusing to be what the world insisted he must remain. To be Black and free in Southampton, to claim your own destiny, was to live every day in defiance of the old order. His ordeal was not over; it had simply changed form.

He found his people scattered—families torn apart, friends vanished, churches and cabins burned or abandoned. But there was also a fierce determination among the newly freed: a hunger to learn, to worship openly, to gather and build anew. Parson became a voice in the settlement, not just for himself but for others. He urged his neighbors to read, to vote, to claim land even when the odds were stacked against them. And in doing so, he built something like hope—a fragile thing, but real.

The Freedmen's Bureau brought a measure of relief. Its agents offered food, shelter, medical care, and schooling—small mercies, but crucial ones. The Bureau's schools, rough and crowded as they were, became a sanctuary. Black children and elders alike crowded into makeshift classrooms, hungry for letters and numbers, for a glimpse of a future not bounded by another man's whim. Parson's own children learned to read by lamplight, their fingers tracing words that had once been forbidden.

But if Reconstruction was a new dawn, it was one ringing with clouds. The old masters did not vanish, nor did their resentments. Former Confederates, stripped of their power but not their pride, lashed out. They used violence, intimidation, and a tangle of new laws—Black Codes, vagrancy statutes, and soon enough, Jim Crow—to claw back what they could not win on the battlefield. Parson saw friends dragged from their homes at night, heard stories of men lynched for claiming the rights supposedly won by war.

Still, he refused to yield. He worked his own patch of land, often at the edge of hunger, and scraped together enough to buy a few acres—land that would, in time, become the anchor for his family. He preached the value of land and schooling, of voting even when the cost was high. He knew true freedom meant more than a slip of paper or a military proclamation; it meant the stubborn, daily work of building something lasting, generation after generation.

"In war," Parson had learned, "the victory is just the blossom, and nothing is more frustrating than a bloom that refuses to morph into some fruit." The end of fighting, for all its fireworks and speeches, was only the start. The real work, the hard, patient work—was turning that fleeting flower of victory into something that could be harvested, something that would feed a family and outlast a season. In Southampton, as all across the South, that fruit proved maddeningly slow to appear.

His journey was marked by small, stubborn triumphs: his children's first schoolbooks, a deed to a patch of stubborn soil, the right to cast a ballot. But each gain came shadowed by new threats. Sharecropping contracts promised independence but delivered debt and dependency. Night riders and white leagues prowled the roads, determined to keep Black ambition in check. Even the churches and schools—those sanctuaries of hope—

were targeted, burned, or shuttered by men who could not abide the sight of Black progress.

And yet, for all the setbacks, he persisted. He gathered his neighbors, organized meetings to explain the rights and responsibilities of citizenship, and taught others how to avoid the snares of unfair labor contracts. He spoke out against discrimination and for a vision of a county where all could thrive—not just the powerful and the white. Slowly, almost imperceptibly, he became a pillar in his community. His voice, once silenced by law and custom, gained weight. His story became a lodestar for others searching for direction in the uncertain new world.

He watched his children take their first hesitant steps into literacy, saw them return from school with heads full of dreams he himself had never dared to consider. He watched his neighbors—some still haunted by memories of the lash—begin to imagine futures for themselves and their families that went beyond mere survival. He saw, too, the cost of these dreams: the violence, the setbacks, the endless struggle to claim what had already been promised.

By the time Parson looked back on his journey, the landscape of Southampton had changed. Churches and schools dotted the countryside, and Black farmers tilled their own land, even if only a few acres. There were, too, the scars: houses burned, men disappeared, rights stripped away as quickly as they were granted. The bloom of victory had not yet ripened into the fruit of justice, but it had not withered completely, either.

For him, the journey was never just about himself. It was about what could be built, brick by brick, lesson by lesson, vote by vote. It was about staking a claim to dignity in a world determined to deny it. It was about a kind of faith—sometimes battered, never quite extinguished—that tomorrow could be better, if only you kept planting, kept teaching, kept fighting.

The years after the war were a time of uneasy possibility. The Constitution was amended, rights were won, but the fight to make them real was just beginning. He saw neighbors fall to violence, saw laws twisted against those they were meant to protect. He buried friends and family, mourned lost opportunities, and yet kept faith with the promise of freedom. The blossom of victory was fragile, easily bruised. But in some seasons, it bore fruit—sweet, hard-won, and even more precious for its rarity.

So, Parson's story—like the story of Reconstruction itself—ends not with triumph, but with endurance. The dream of a just and equal Southampton flickered but did not die. The fruit of freedom grew slowly, sometimes stunted, sometimes stolen, but always replanted by those determined to claim their place in the world.

The years rolled on, and with them came new faces and old fears. Parson watched as some neighbors, freshly emancipated, tried to put distance between themselves and the men who had once owned them. Others, unable or unwilling to leave, struck uneasy bargains—sharecropping contracts inked with hope but sealed by necessity. He knew those contracts well. He had seen how a season's bad luck could wipe out a year's labor, how a crooked tally at the general store could bind a man tighter than any chain.

Yet there was a stubborn solidarity in the settlement. Folks pooled what little they had, built cabins from scrap, shared seeds, passed around books and newsprint until the pages grew soft from too many hands. Parson's cabin became a gathering place—sometimes for prayer, sometimes for debate, sometimes just for rest. He welcomed those who came seeking advice, or simply a moment's warmth from his hearth. He listened more than he spoke, but when he did, his words carried the weight of someone who had lost much and clawed back what little could be salvaged.

He never forgot those first days after the war, when the Freedmen's Bureau agents appeared, offering not just food and shelter but the faintest outline of new possibilities. Parson never romanticized the Bureau—he had seen its limits, its failures, and the resentment it stirred among the old guard—but he could not ignore what it had meant. The Bureau's schoolhouse taught his daughters to read, its field agents helped him negotiate his first fair contract. There was dignity in those small victories. They did not erase the past, but they offered a path forward.

Other victories proved more elusive. The right to vote was a right in theory, but in practice, it was a gauntlet—one lined with threats, bribes, and the ever-present risk of violence. Parson urged his neighbors to register anyway, to show up at the polls even when the outcome seemed foregone. Sometimes they left with ink-stained fingers and a fleeting sense of power; other times, they left with bruises and a warning not to come back.

Each election felt like a test of endurance. The act of voting could feel almost futile, a gesture that changed nothing. But he insisted it mattered. "If nothing else," he told his son, "it's a way of saying we're still here. That we won't be erased." He never stopped believing in the slow work of democracy, even when it seemed the world was set against him.

There were, of course, men like Jacob Williams—former enslavers now reduced by war and emancipation to something smaller and meaner than they had been. Jacob tried to hold on to the old ways, to reassert his authority over Black laborers with the Vagrancy Act and other tools of the new Southern order. But Parson, newly married and determined to claim a life on his own terms, refused to be bound by another man's nostalgia. He built his home in the Black settlement, far from Jacob's gaze. Others followed, and the landscape began to shift, if only a little.

The transition was not smooth. Jacob's resentment simmered, and labor disputes flared. Parson remembered the year when Black laborers, tired of Jacob's terms, simply refused to work his fields. The crops withered in the ground, a silent testament to the power of collective action. It was a small rebellion, easily overlooked in the larger story of the South, but for Parson and his neighbors, it was proof that things could change. Not easily, not completely, but change all the same.

Everywhere, the patterns of the old world collided with the demands of the new. The law said one thing, the county another. "Whites Only" signs appeared like blisters on the landscape—at the train depot, outside the courthouse, above the counters of the shops. They were daily reminders that the war's end had not brought true peace, only a fragile ceasefire. Parson learned to navigate these barriers, teaching his children to do the same, but he never stopped resenting the quiet violence of exclusion.

He saw, too, the efforts of Northern teachers—white and Black, men and women—who came South to teach the newly freed. Their presence was sometimes a blessing, sometimes a provocation. In Southampton, as elsewhere, schools became battlegrounds. Black parents fought for their children's right to learn, even as white mobs threatened to burn the buildings down. Parson's oldest daughter, Ruth, recited her lessons in a whisper, always listening for the sound of trouble at the door.

There were moments of grace, too. Parson attended his daughter's school exhibition—watched her stand before a crowded room, her voice clear and proud as she read from the Psalms. For a moment, the past seemed to recede. Yet even then, the future felt uncertain. The next morning brought news of another lynching, another family driven from their land under cover of darkness.

In war, the victory is just the blossom, and nothing is more frustrating than a bloom that refuses to morph into some fruit. He felt this acutely. The battles had ended, the banners lowered, but the work of turning promise into reality—of coaxing fruit from stubborn ground—had barely begun. The blossom drew crowds, inspired speeches, but fruit required patience, tending, and a kind of faith in seasons yet to come. The

South was full of blossoms, he thought—parades, proclamations, constitutional amendments—but too few fruits. Too little justice, too little peace.

He watched old enemies return to power, sometimes with new faces, always with the same eyes. The rise of Jim Crow, the tightening grip of segregation and disenfranchisement, made a mockery of the victories so hard-won. Sometimes he wondered if the old world had ever really ended, or if it had just changed its clothes. The dream of equality felt as distant as ever, but he refused to let go. He taught his children that freedom, once claimed, could not be surrendered. Not truly. Not forever.

His faith was tested daily. He saw Black teachers harassed, Black voters turned away, Black churches burned. He buried friends who had dared to dream too boldly, who had paid with their lives for wanting just a taste of what white men took for granted. Yet he kept building, kept teaching, kept gathering his people—if not for justice now, then for the hope of it tomorrow.

By the end of Reconstruction, he had won some victories that could not be taken from him. He owned his land and had buried his feet deep in its soil. He had secured his children's future, not just with deeds and papers, but with knowledge— with the stubborn, subversive power of literacy. His family had survived, and that in itself was a quiet miracle.

But the price was steep. The fruit of freedom, when it appeared, was often small, bruised, and quickly snatched away. He knew this, but he also knew that the alternative—surrender, silence, forgetting—was unthinkable. So he endured. For his children, for his neighbors, for the memory of those who had never lived to see the blossom, let alone the fruit.

In the end, his greatest legacy was not the land he owned or the votes he cast, but the example he set: to keep reaching, keep hoping, even when the world refused to yield. To believe that, with enough patience and enough courage, the blossom might yet become fruit.

This was the paradox of freedom after war: it was given but never guaranteed; promised, but always in need of defending. In the settlements, in the schools, in the fields, Parson and his neighbors did the work that the war had only begun. They planted, they taught, they voted. They waited for the fruit.

Parson's story was not the only one unfolding in the patchwork of Southampton County. Others carried their own burdens, their own hard-won hopes, and losses. Joseph and Henry, returned from service, found the county changed in ways both glaring and invisible. They had fought with the Union, worn blue, marched beneath the flag that promised liberty. But when the fighting was done, they returned to a home where old hatreds simmered beneath a veneer of law. They brought back more than uniforms, they brought back eyes that had seen beyond the plantation, minds that had learned to question, hands that no longer trembled when grasping a ballot or a pen.

Joseph and Henry, too, refused the sharecropping system when they could. They pooled their savings, bought a wedge of land so narrow it barely held a house and a garden, but it was theirs. On Sunday afternoons, you could find them sitting side by side on the porch, shirtsleeves rolled, talking softly about the world beyond Southampton, about the taste of real wages, about the promise of voting. It was not the life they had imagined, but it was a start—a stem pushing up from stony ground, stubborn and green.

Solomon and Louisa, older now, watched their children and grandchildren with a wary hopefulness. They had come of age in a world where reading was a crime for people like them. Now, they watched the next generation clutching dog-eared spellers, reciting lines from the Bible. Louisa, who'd once taught her children by firelight, pressing their fingers to the shapes of letters scratched in the dirt, saw the hope and the cost of formal schooling. The schools were segregated, under-funded, sometimes little more than shacks, but inside, the hum of learning was a kind of quiet rebellion. The world was shifting, even if only by inches.

The church stood at the center of everything—a place of solace, a well of resistance. It was where Parson and the others gathered to plan, to grieve, to sing, to remember. The church was more than a building, more than a pulpit: it was a shelter against the storms of white violence, a forge for leaders, a place to imagine new possibilities. The preacher might visit only once a month, but in his absence, lay leaders like Parson kept the flame alive. The church taught more than scripture; it taught dignity, strategy, and the long view.

In many ways, the Black settlement became its own society. Barred from white businesses, Black men and women built their own: seamstresses, barbers, cobblers, teachers, preachers, and, for the lucky few, landowners. The entrepreneurial class was small, battered by the shifting tides of white hostility, but it was there, and it mattered. It gave young people a glimpse of something different—a world where Black ambition was not always met with a closed door or a raised fist.

Yet every step forward was met with resistance. The "Whites Only" signs grew bolder, more brazen. Vagrancy laws, so loosely written they could mean anything, were used as weapons—tools to push Black people off land, into jail, back into debt, back into submission. Parson saw neighbors rounded up for imagined crimes, forced to work fields under the guise of "public order." The clang of chains was gone, but the sound of injustice lingered, echoing in the hollows of the county.

Still, there were days when hope outpaced fear. Parson's son, Samuel, learned to write his name with a flourish. Joseph's daughter, Lottie, earned a certificate from the Freedmen's school. Solomon's grandson, born in freedom, grew up never knowing the taste of the lash. These were the fruits Parson spoke of—modest, vulnerable, easily bruised, but fruits all the same. Each one was a quiet rebuke to the world that said Black people could not, would not, should not thrive.

But the world did not change fast enough. In the years after Reconstruction, the old powers regrouped, reasserted themselves. Jim Crow crept in, sly at first, then overt. Ballots disappeared, violence returned, and the laws bent themselves backward to reassert the color line. Parson saw the dream of true equality wither on the vine, saw neighbors forced to leave, saw schools shuttered and churches burned. The fruit, once within reach, was snatched away repeatedly.

"In war, the victory is just the blossom," Parson would say, "but here, every spring, the frost comes late. The blooms are bright, but the fruit—if it comes at all—is small, and bitter, and fleeting." He said it not to discourage, but to steel the hearts of those around him. To remind them that history was not a straight path, and that the work of freedom was never finished.

Beyond Southampton, the pattern repeated. Across the South, men and women who had tasted liberty found themselves hemmed in by new walls. The violence was sometimes open—a lynching, a pogrom, a night of fire and broken glass. Sometimes, it was quieter: a job denied, a contract broken, a school closed for "repairs" that never ended. The hope of Reconstruction, so bright at first, dulled with every setback.

But there was something irrepressible in people who had survived centuries of bondage. Parson saw it in the way his neighbors came together after every loss, rebuilt after every fire, taught their children to read after every school was closed. He saw it in the quiet dignity with which men and women bore the insults and injuries of daily life, refusing to surrender what had been so painfully won.

The world outside Southampton County did not always understand this resilience. Politicians in Washington argued over appropriations, over the reach of federal power, and over the meaning of citizenship. Presidents came and went. Some, like Grant, tried to protect the fragile gains of Reconstruction. Others, like Andrew Johnson, seemed determined to undo them at every turn, pardoning former Confederates, vetoing protective laws, urging a return to the old order.

Parson, for his part, paid little mind to the comings and goings of distant men. His world was the county, the land, the church, the schoolhouse. But he understood, as few others did, just how fragile freedom could be. He watched the passage of the Fifteenth Amendment with hope, saw men and women line up to vote for the first time, and then saw those same rights eroded, year by year, law by law. He watched as Northern interest waned, as Southern resistance hardened, as the country turned its gaze elsewhere.

He knew, too, that the struggle was not just for himself, or for his children, but for those yet unborn. The world he was building—slowly, painfully, against the grain—might one day bear fruit he would never live to taste. That was the hope, and the sorrow, at the heart of his journey.

The blossom of victory, the promise of freedom were not enough. It was the fruit that mattered: land owned, children educated, dignity preserved. And even when the harvest was meager, Parson kept planting, kept tending, kept hoping.

Time passed. Children grew. Old men faded. The dream that had burned so hot in the first days of freedom cooled, yet it never vanished. Some mornings, Parson would rise before the sun and walk the rows of his small field, feeling the earth with his hands, thinking about all that had been gained and lost. He had become, without ever intending it, a witness to the full arc of a country's experiment—an experiment that had promised much and delivered only what it absolutely could not deny.

He often thought in those quiet hours, about the blossom and the fruit. In war, the victory is just the blossom, he would remind himself, but the work—the true work—is coaxing that blossom, fragile and beautiful, into something that will last. A blossom can fool the eye, can make you think the season has changed for good. But unless it is tended, unless the soil is right and the weather holds, that blossom will shrivel, and the promise will go to rot. He had seen too many promises wither.

In the decades that followed, as Reconstruction was quietly strangled and Jim Crow's shadow spread across the land, Parson and his neighbors had to learn how to survive not just disappointment, but betrayal. The country that had demanded their loyalty, their blood, their hope, seemed always to stop short of full embrace. The victories of the battlefield faded like old banners; the real test came after, when the world lost interest and the work got hard.

It was only much later—years after Parson was gone, after his children had grown and scattered—that historians would start to draw comparisons between the broken promises of Reconstruction and the triumphs of another rebuilding: the Marshall Plan. Parson never heard of the Marshall Plan; the name would have meant nothing to him. But the lesson, the contrast, was plain to anyone who cared to see.

In the wake of World War II, the United States poured money, expertise, and energy into the ruined nations of Europe. Teams of experts, rebuilt factories, funded new schools, rewrote constitutions. And they did it not grudgingly, not in fits and starts, but with a relentless, sustained commitment. The victors did not just plant a blossom and walk away, they stayed to ensure the fruit would come and come again.

Southampton County, and the South as a whole, never got that kind of care. The freedmen were given rights on paper, but too often left to fend for themselves in a landscape hostile to their very existence. The army withdrew. The schools closed. The laws bent to the will of those who had never accepted defeat. What could have been a true new birth—an American Marshall Plan—was left to wither, sabotaged by indifference, by racism, by the unspoken belief that some blossoms were not worth the trouble of fruit.

Parson's people had been offered emancipation, then left to navigate the minefield of freedom with little more than hope and stubbornness. The money that rebuilt Europe was never spent in Southampton, or Selma, or Memphis. The experts who shaped German democracy never came to teach in the one-room schoolhouses of the South. The commitment lasted only as long as the headlines, and then it was gone. In the fields, in the churches, in the tiny, fragile banks and budding businesses, Black Americans were forced to make do with less—always less.

And yet—they endured. Parson's story did not end with despair. The fruit was slow, often bitter, sometimes stolen, but never entirely absent. The lessons he taught his children—about dignity, about community, about the long fight—were handed down, year by year, until they found new expression in new generations. The struggle continued, changed shape, found new voices. The church bells still rang on Sundays, the schools still opened their doors, the fields still bore crops.

Looking back, it's easy to see what might have been—how a true commitment to Reconstruction, on par with the Marshall Plan, could have transformed not just the South, but the whole nation. It's easy to imagine a world in which the blossom did not die on the branch, in which the fruit was plentiful and sweet, in which the promises of the war were not just words, but lived realities for all.

But history, Parson knew, was never so generous. It yields only what is demanded of it, and sometimes not even that. The victories of war are only beginnings, bright and brief. The real challenge is the patient, back-breaking labor of turning victory into justice, promise into reality, blossoming into fruit.

Parson's life was spent in that labor, and though he did not live to see its full reward, he left behind a legacy of endurance, of hope in the face of heartbreak. His children, and their children after them, walked the same roads he had walked, faced the same old hatreds in new forms. But they also carried forward the stubborn belief that the fruit, though delayed, would come.

Sometimes on quiet evenings, Parson would stand at the edge of his field and watch the sun set over Southampton. The air would be heavy with the scent of earth and grass, the sound of children's laughter drifting through the trees. In those moments, the world felt balanced between what was and what might still be. The blossom was still there, fragile and bright, and the fruit—though far off—seemed, for a moment, almost within reach.

The story of Parson, of Joseph and Henry, of Solomon and Louisa, is not a story of defeat. It is a story of persistence, of small victories, of seeds planted in rocky soil. It is a story of the long, hard road from promise to fulfillment—a road that winds through heartbreak and hope, through seasons of blossom and seasons of fruit.

It is a story still being written.

About the Author

COL David J. Mason, U.S. Army, Retired, is Owner and Founder of HMG ePublishing, LLC, and the great-grandson of Parson Sykes.

Mr. Mason became interested in the history of the Sykes family early in life while attending family reunions and hearing stories of his mother's ancestors from Southampton County, Virginia. The family descended from Louisa Williams Sykes, an enslaved Black American matriarch who had lived on Jacob Williams' farm located on Barrow Road in the Cross Keys neighborhood.

For over 150 years, Parson Sykes' descendants have passed down stories and adventures from Parson's early life at family reunions, holiday meals, weddings, and other gatherings where the ancestors met. During the Civil War, Parson and his brothers, Joseph and Henry, made a challenging escape from bondage to reach Fort Monroe in early December 1864. After enlistment, they performed successful combat military duty with the XXV Corps, USCT.

Intrigued by what he heard at a family gathering, David researched the military service of Parson, Joseph, Henry, and others. He published *The Self-Liberation of Parson Sykes*, a documentary novel based on the true self-liberation ordeal and actual events drawn from a variety of sources, including published materials and family chronicles. In the trilogy, Parson and Jacob Williams are confronted with opposing views on the contentious moral issues of enslavement, secession, and emancipation, which led directly to war and Reconstruction. This work follows Parson's life, starting with his enslavement, followed by his enlistment in the Union Army, and concluding with his return to Jacob Williams' farm as a free man.

This is the story of Parson's quest for practical freedom against the immense forces of systemic racism and a nation struggling to live up to its promises. On April 3, 1865, units of the Army XXV Corps were among the first to enter the city that for the past four years had been the capital of the Confederacy, where Parson arrived at his destination. After the Civil War, the army ordered the XXV Corps to Texas for border duty. Upon returning to Southampton County during the turbulent Reconstruction era, he confronts a society rife with racial violence and political betrayal.

Mr. Mason is the author of the Environmental Compliance Tool Kit (Thompson Publishing Group, 1994) and the Internet Marketing Tool Kit (HMG ePublishing, 2006). He holds a Master of Science degree in chemistry from Hampton University in Virginia and a Bachelor of Science degree in chemistry from Norfolk State University. He is a graduate of the Army War College.

Acknowledgments

Over the three years it took me to complete this trilogy, family members provided me with help and encouragement in writing The Self-Liberation of Parson Sykes. Foremost, I am indebted to my incredible wife, Paige Hinton-Mason. I want to thank Paige for her steadfast patience, lively discussions, and loving encouragement. Her confidence in me has been the foundation on which my efforts to complete this book arose. Her tolerance, support, editing, and suggestions for improving the manuscript helped inspire literary practices that I never knew I needed. It is because of her input that I have a written story to share with my family and friends, which did not previously exist.

I am eternally grateful to my brother and sister. Among them is my sister Mary M. Sumner, who rose to the level of contributing editor for this project. She deserves much appreciation for her suggestions for improving the manuscript and for shepherding it through multiple drafts until it was ready for publication. Her encouragement and editing skills, which included grammar and content editing to ensure quality, made this book possible. Thank you so much for your continual help with this book.

And to my brother, Gilbert, who often served more like a contributing editor to me than a mentor. As contributing editor, he exchanged storyline ideas, advised on content for the book, collected and forwarded historical articles, took photographs of the Sykes farm and other extinguishing landmarks. In particular, he provided the photo of the cotton field featured on the book's cover. Besides this, I owe thanks to him for the trips he made to government facilities to research and collect historical information and records that supported the family's oral chronicles, which helped to make this project possible. He utilized a variety of helpful research tools, including publicly available archives, visiting libraries, and archives and record depositories.

I am especially grateful to my cousin, Rosa Sykes Wynne, for her exemplary recollection of anecdotes presented at family reunions and gatherings. Her editorial contribution included documenting Parson and his descendants, which were valuable resources for developing content for the trilogy. She provided a first-hand description of life in Southampton County and shared memories of family history, celebratory events, and traditions. Thank you so much for your help in memorializing our ancestral roots.

I am grateful to my grandson, Chase Neighbors, for offering his likeness of Parson Sykes on the cover of the book in civilian. Using his image was essential to recreating the appearance of Parson at the end of the Reconstruction Era. Thank you for the reenactment image and visage of the book.

While writing the book, other family members provided me with help and encouragement. I am also indebted to them for endorsing and supporting my work. Among these are aunts and uncles, nieces, nephews, cousins, and in-laws. Special thanks to my Aunt Marie Sykes for her extensive phone conversations about Southampton County and our family history. In addition, thanks to her and Uncle Lloyd Sykes for hosting and contributing to our ongoing tradition of family reunions.

Special thanks to researcher Leslie Anderson, MSLS, for her detailed examination of the civilian and military experiences of those who served in the 1st Cavalry Regiment, USCT. Her investigation provided a tremendous amount of information about Parson and his brothers. Her research also established the impact of Reconstruction on the civilian lives of these soldiers and their families after the war. For example, it revealed the struggles Black families faced in securing pensions for veterans and their widows, facing scrutiny and denial based on legal and societal interpretations of marriage and relationships.

Finally, among the many debts I owe in developing this book is to Daniel W. Crofts. In his book, Old Southampton: Politics and Society in a Virginia County, 1834-1869, he included evidence of the military service of three enslaved brothers, Harrison, Joseph, and Henry Williams. This passage in Crofts' book resembled our oral family history of how Parson Sykes escaped enslavement, with which I was familiar. It induced me to research the brothers in the passage. Subsequently, I discovered that Harrison Williams was an alias that my great-grandfather, Parson Sykes, assumed after he fled Southampton, County. The diligent research reflected in Crofts' works has made mine possible.

Glossary

Abraham Lincoln: 16th President of the United States. In the world of Parson, Lincoln's leadership during the Civil War and his push to abolish slavery set the national stage for the struggles and hopes of Black Americans fighting for freedom. His presidency is both a distant power and a looming presence over every enslaved person plotting escape.

Andrew Johnson: 17th President of the United States. He favored the quick restoration of the seceded states to the Union without protection for the former slaves. This led to conflict with the Republican-dominated Congress, culminating in his impeachment by the House of Representatives in 1868. He was acquitted in the Senate by one vote.

Black Codes: Laws passed in the South immediately after the Civil War. In the novel, the Black Codes are the invisible chains meant to keep newly freed people in conditions barely better than slavery, trapping characters like Parson and his community in a system rigged against their self-determination.

Civil Rights Act of 1964: A landmark civil rights and labor law in the United States that outlawed discrimination based on race, color, religion, sex, national origin, and later sexual orientation and gender identity. It prohibits unequal application of voter registration requirements, racial segregation in schools and public accommodations, and employment discrimination. The act "remains one of the most significant legislative achievements in American history".

Compromise of 1877: The backroom deal that ended Reconstruction by pulling federal troops out of the South. For the novel, this marks the moment hope dims for many freed people, as protection vanishes and white supremacy surges back, making Parson's quest for dignity even riskier.

Confederate Lost Cause Movement: An American pseudo-historical, negationist ideology that advocates the belief that the cause of the Confederate States during the American Civil War was a just and heroic one. This ideology has furthered the belief that enslavement was just and moral because the enslaved were happy, even grateful, and it also brought economic prosperity. The notion was used to perpetuate racism and racist power structures during the Jim Crow era in the American South. It emphasizes the supposed chivalric virtues of the antebellum South.

Cotton Gin: Invented in 1793, the cotton gin revolutionized cotton production, which in turn fueled slavery in the South for many years. In the novel, the cotton gin is less a technological marvel than the engine of an economy built on stolen labor—its legacy woven into every field, every back bent in the blistering sun.

Dred Scott v. Sandford Decision: Landmark decision of the U.S. Supreme Court in which the Court held that the U.S. Constitution was not meant to include American citizenship for Black people, regardless of whether they were enslaved or free, and so the rights and privileges that the Constitution confers upon American citizens could not apply to them. Dred Scott was born into slavery in Southampton County, Virginia, around 1799.

Emancipation Proclamation: Issued by President Abraham Lincoln, the Proclamation declared that as of January 1, 1863, all enslaved people in the states currently engaged in rebellion against the Union "shall be then, thenceforward, and forever free." Lincoln did not actually free any of the approximately four million men, women, and children held in enslavement in the United States when he signed the formal Emancipation Proclamation. The document applied only to enslaved people in the Confederacy, and not to those in the border states that remained loyal to the Union.

Fifteenth Amendment: The 15th Amendment was ratified on February 3, 1870. It states that "The right of citizens of the United States to vote shall not be denied or abridged by the United States, or by any State, on account of race, color, or previous condition of servitude."

Fourteenth Amendment: The 14th Amendment to the U.S. Constitution, ratified in 1868, granted citizenship to all persons born or naturalized in the United States—including former enslaved people—and guaranteed all citizens "equal protection of the laws."

Freedmen's Bureau: Formally known as the Bureau of Refugees, Freedmen, and Abandoned Lands, was established in 1865 by Congress to help millions of former black slaves and poor whites in the South in the aftermath of the Civil War. The Freedmen's Bureau provided food, housing, and medical aid, established schools, and offered legal assistance. It also attempted to settle former slaves on land that had been confiscated or abandoned during the war. However, the Bureau was prevented from fully carrying out its programs due to a shortage of funds and personnel, as well as the complexities of race and Reconstruction politics.

Kansas-Nebraska Act: 1854 law allowing settlers of a territory to decide on slavery, leading to violence. The act's aftermath shapes the borders and attitudes in Parson's world, where the question of slavery's future is always present and always personal.

Military-Civil Affairs: The activities of a commander that establish, maintain, influence, or exploit relations between military forces, governmental and non-governmental civilian organizations, and authorities.

Missouri Compromise: United States federal legislation that stopped northern attempts to prohibit the expansion of enslavement by admitting Missouri as a pro-enslavement state in exchange for legislation that prohibited enslavement north of the thirty-six-degree-30-minute parallel except for Missouri. The 16th United States Congress passed the legislation on March 3, 1820, and President James Monroe signed it on March 6, 1820.

Pogrom: Organized massacre of a group, often with official support. In the context of the novel, the threat of white mob violence—sanctioned or ignored by those in power—hangs over every Black family daring to claim their rights.

Radical Republicans: A faction in Congress pushing for full rights for Black Americans and strict terms for Southern states rejoining the Union. Their political battles shape the opportunities and risks for characters in the novel, offering moments of hope amid backlash.

Raid on Harper's Ferry: An effort by abolitionist John Brown, from October 16 to 18, 1859, to initiate an anti-enslavement revolt in Southern states by taking over the United States arsenal at Harpers Ferry, Virginia. It has been called the dress rehearsal for, or tragic prelude to, the Civil War.

Sharecropping: After the Civil War, former slaves sought jobs, and planters sought laborers. The absence of cash or an independent credit system led to the creation of sharecropping. Sharecropping is a system where the landlord/planter allows a tenant to use the land in exchange for a share of the crop. This encouraged tenants to work to produce the largest harvest they could, ensuring they would remain tied to the land and unlikely to leave for other opportunities.

Special: Field Order 15: Also known as "40 Acres and a Mule", Union General William Tecumseh Sherman issued this field order in January 1865. The order confiscated 400,000 acres of land along the Atlantic coast of South Carolina, Georgia, and Florida. It divided the land into parcels of not more than forty acres, on which approximately 18,000 formerly enslaved families and other Black people living in the area were to be settled.

Thirteenth Amendment: Passed by Congress on January 31, 1865, and ratified on December 6, 1865, the 13th amendment abolished enslavement in the United States and provides that "Neither enslavement nor involuntary servitude, except as a punishment for crime whereof the party shall have been duly convicted, shall exist within the United States, or any place subject to their jurisdiction.".

Three-Fifths Compromise: A compromise agreement between delegates from the Northern and Southern states at the United States Constitutional Convention (1787) that stipulated three-fifths of the enslaved population would be counted for determining direct taxation and representation in the House of Representatives.

Voting Rights Act of 1965: A landmark piece of federal legislation in the United States that prohibits racial discrimination in voting.